WHEN THE THE MOUNTAINS ROARED

JESS BUTTERWORTH

Orion

ORION CHILDREN'S BOOKS

First published in Great Britain in 2018
by Hodder and Stoughton

1 3 5 7 9 10 8 6 4 2

Text copyright © Jess Butterworth, 2018

A CIP catalogue record for this book
is available from the British Library.

ISBN 978 1 51010 211 8

Typeset by Input Data Services Ltd, Somerset

Printed and bound in Great Britain by CPI Group (UK) Ltd, Croydon CR0 4YY

The paper and board used in this book are made
from wood from responsible sources.

Orion Children's Books
An imprint of
Hachette Children's Group
Part of Hodder and Stoughton
Carmelite House
50 Victoria Embankment
London EC4Y 0DZ

An Hachette UK Company

www.hachette.co.uk
www.hachettechildrens.co.uk

To my Grandma,
who travelled from Australia to India in the 60s
with a border collie and a kangaroo in tow

I duck low to the ground and creep forwards, following the two men and the boy ahead. The trees rustle and dappled light flickers around me. I step as silently as I can, avoiding twigs and crisp leaves. The group stops, and I dart behind a tree. I can't be seen. They have guns.

I flatten myself against the trunk and peer around it. They're gathered by a thick tree, examining the base.

I know what they're looking for: some trace of the leopard. But leopards are elusive. Their spotted coats and padded feet allow them to hide in shadows. There are only five ways to find a leopard: you can track their paw prints; follow their scratches and scrapes; look for their scat; discover their scent markings; and listen for other animals' alarm calls.

'Over there,' says the boy, pointing ahead. He raises his finger to his lips.

They move on, quieter and quicker.

I wait until they're out of sight then dash to the trunk they were inspecting.

A line of ants runs down it. Next to them, etched into the bark, are claw marks. I touch the scratches. They're fresh. A leopard was here recently. I sniff. I don't detect a spray odour. It's a good sign that the claw marks are a few days old. I turn back in the direction of the men and hope with all my might that the leopard is far away by now.

I sneak after the group again and soon catch glimpses of them through the trees. The forest throbs with the buzz of cicadas and chirp of birds. As I step over a fern, I slip on a rock and scrape my palms breaking my fall. I freeze on the ground.

Did they hear me?

Between the fern leaves ahead I spot their legs. They've stopped in the path. My heart pounds. I imagine what I'll say if I'm caught. Or worse, I realise they could think I'm a leopard and shoot me.

Maybe I should shout now.

But I stay silent and through the parted fern, I watch. They're not turning to look at me; they're staring at something on the ground.

I sink lower and wait.

The men peer into the undergrowth around them, before heading off to the left, in a new direction.

I dart to the place where they'd stopped. There are paw prints in the dirt, pointing in the direction the men went. They're about eight centimetres long. The main pad has three lobes on the back of it. Four toe prints with no claws sit above the pad. They're lightly imprinted in the earth. It definitely belongs to a leopard; they tread gently. The back paw print shines. I bend and touch it. It's sticky and I pull my hand back.

My fingers come away deep red.

My breath catches.

Blood.

I wipe my shaky hands on my trousers. There's a leopard out there, injured. And I have to find it before they do.

CHAPTER ONE

Australia: Two Months Earlier

I know something's wrong as soon as I step through the front door.

Everything we own is scattered across the living room floor in a sea of clothes, books and household objects. The living room rug is rolled up, the shelves are empty, and even the plates from the kitchen dresser are stacked up on the carpet next to it.

For a split second I think we've been burgled. But then Dad comes clomping down the stairs in his boots, with an armful of coats, and Grandma enters from the kitchen. Polly, our border collie, leaps up at me, rests her front paws on my chest and licks my face.

'What happened?' I ask, pushing Polly down and stroking her. I let my school backpack thud to the floor.

'We're moving,' says Dad. His mouth is hard.

'Moving?' I tilt my head to the side. 'Why?'

When no one says anything, I ask, 'Where?'

'India,' says Grandma. She rests her hand on my shoulder and squeezes it. 'Where your dad and I were born.'

I stare at them both, open-mouthed. 'We can't.'

'I've got a new job at a hotel there,' says Dad.

My heart races. 'What about this job?' I ask. 'This hotel?'

'It's a great opportunity, Ruby,' Dad says,

speaking to the coat he's folding into a box, rather than to me. 'I've been headhunted to be the manager of a new hotel opening soon.'

I look at Grandma.

'Think how much fun it will be to explore and photograph a new place,' she says to me. 'Besides, we want to show you what India is like. It will be an adventure.'

I can tell there's more they're not saying. It's the way Grandma's voice falters, the suddenness of the packing, and how Dad can't keep his eyes on mine.

Anger shoots through my body.

'What if I don't want to go?' I ask, my voice rising. 'Can I stay here?'

'It's not up for discussion, Ruby.' His voice is low and grim. Dad never shouts when he's cross or worried. 'We're leaving in the morning.'

There's a silence that follows.

I repeat his words over and over in my mind.

Something's wrong. I know it.

Hurt prickles down the back of my throat that they didn't talk to me first, that I don't have any say in it or even a choice.

'I'm not coming!' I yell to hide how upset I am, and storm into the kitchen.

The table is buried under glass cases filled with the snakes' skins that Mum studied, next to books about snake habitat and behaviour. Mum was an ophiologist. I slide my hand across the case with Caspar inside, a taxidermy emerald tree python. My fingers leave a line in the dust.

My camera is on the side of the table. I grab it and stride through to the garden. I sit on the edge of the porch, hugging my knees. Gazing out over the red desert, I spot dingoes on the mounds in the distance. Polly pads out of the house and lies down next to me, panting in the heat.

I won't go. There's nothing they can do to make me. Emily and I are doing a joint art project for school next week. It's her birthday next month and we had plans to go camping together over summer. I can't miss all that.

Grandma joins me and pulls up a rocking chair. 'Here,' she says, leaning in and passing me a slice of watermelon. My favourite fruit. Grandma's turquoise bangle gleams in the sun against her brown skin. Her breath smells of barbeque sauce.

'I'm not hungry.' I turn my back to her.

A flock of galahs fly past in a flash of pink. They land and rest on the closest eucalyptus tree. I lift the camera from around my neck and snap a picture of them.

We moved houses often when I was younger. Mum's snake research took her to different universities and Dad managed hotels up and down the country. But when they found this hotel, miles from anything in the outback, they fell in love with it and stayed. I thought we'd live here for ever.

But then I thought Mum would be here for ever too.

'Why does Dad really want to leave?' I ask, lowering the camera. I turn to face Grandma and meet her deep eyes. 'You can tell me.'

Grandma looks at me and wrinkles gather in the centre of her forehead. 'There are too many memories here for him, perhaps.'

I shake my head. 'That's not it.' I know Dad. Every week he shows me the roses Mum planted, before we sit on the bench she used to watch the sunset from, and eat strawberry ice cream. It was her favourite flavour. He *loves* those memories.

'I think you'll enjoy it in India,' says Grandma.

I sigh.

'It takes courage to start something new. And you, Ruby, are the most courageous little girl I know.'

'I'm actually twelve now,' I reply, digging a hole in the dirt with my big toe. I'd never let anyone but Grandma call me little. I turn to her. 'You can't make me want to go.'

'I know,' she says.

It doesn't loosen the growing knot in my stomach. I clutch the small stone threaded on a string around my neck. It isn't a precious stone or anything, but I found it out walking with Mum, and that makes it priceless.

CHAPTER TWO

Darkness

I'm still sitting on the porch when Dad drives the ute to the back of the house and loads Grandma's suitcase into the bed of it.

Back in the kitchen, he removes Caspar, the taxidermy python, from the display case and packs him, leaving all the other snake things behind. He catches me watching from the porch.

'There's only enough room for us to bring one suitcase each,' he says. 'Can I help you pack?'

I shake my head and go to my bedroom, turn my music up and ignore him and Grandma.

We don't have that many belongings – when the hotel guests stopped coming, Dad sold almost everything, even the piano. Still, they stay up late into the evening packing.

Near ten o'clock there's a loud knock on the door and Dad enters. He turns the music off and perches at the edge of my bed, on Mum's patchwork quilt. 'You can be angry at me all you want but you still have to pack.'

He waits.

I remain silent and seething.

'I don't have time for this, Ruby,' he says, pressing his palm against his forehead.

'Go away,' I say and bury my head under my pillow.

'I'll pack for you if I have to. We're leaving in the morning,' says Dad.

Outside, a distant car engine rumbles. I lift my head. From the window, I see a tiny dot of light moving through the darkness towards the house. Our driveway stretches for miles. We haven't had any guests or visitors for at least a few months now.

Dad's body stiffens. He runs to the window and yanks the curtains closed. Flattening himself against the wall, he lifts the curtain slightly and peers outside. 'It's too late,' he says.

Grandma bursts into the room. 'Have you seen? They're here.'

'Who?' I ask, at the same time as Grandma asks, 'What do we do?'

'We go now,' says Dad.

'Who's here?' I ask again.

He ignores my question. 'Get Polly on her lead,' he says.

'Quickly,' says Grandma, ushering me towards the stairs.

'But I haven't packed yet.'

'Just grab what you can,' says Dad.

'But . . .' My voice trails off and I stand there swaying, my heart pounding.

'Ruby. We need to leave.' He raises his voice. There's a fear in his eyes that makes me listen and jerks my body into action.

'Don't be seen in the windows,' he says.

Why is Dad afraid of them?

11

'Ruby!' hisses Grandma up the stairs. 'Quickly now.'

I dart to my cupboard. I only have seconds to decide what to take. I snatch up some jeans and a few tops. I know it's hot in India.

I stuff my mini torches into my pocket. I'll need those. And my camera. I stop in the doorway, rush back, and grab a photo of me and Mum from the bedside table, along with Mum's quilt.

With my arms full, I sprint down the stairs, leaving everything else behind.

My whole life.

Grandma fastens Polly's lead and passes it to me. Dad guides us silently out of the back door. The night air is still except for bats flitting in and out of the trees and the sound of the car driving towards our house. The building blocks us from sight but I still see flashes from the moving car's lights in the distance.

We have to cross the back garden to reach the ute. I stamp my feet instinctively to warn any snakes that we're coming.

'Not tonight,' whispers Dad. 'Tonight we take our chances with the snakes.'

We follow each other in a line. The night's darkness wraps itself around me, squeezing my insides. My breath quickens. There are three things I've been scared of since I lost Mum. The first is darkness.

I reach out to grab the back of Grandma's coat with one hand. My jacket rustles. My other fingers find the torch in my pocket and grip it nervously.

Polly's ears prick up. 'Shh,' I whisper to her. 'Quiet now.' She crouches low to the ground, staying close to my side.

Dad opens the ute doors and we pile inside one after the other, and sit in a row in the front. Polly, excited by a night outing, wags her tail at me before jumping on to my lap. We pull the door gently closed and it clicks shut.

Dad starts the engine. It's loud at first then settles to a hum.

Did they hear?

He keeps the headlights turned off.

I glance at the moving lights. They must be only a few minutes away now.

'Everyone hold on,' says Dad. 'We're going off road.'

He drives in darkness through the bush, down one of the trails we haven't used in a long time. It's overgrown and bumpy. The moon casts just enough light to see the shadows of the ditches.

We meet eyes in the rear-view mirror.

'Don't worry,' says Dad. 'I know these paths like the back of my hand.'

We bump over rocks. The ute tilts to the side as the wheels spin slowly up a verge.

I turn and stare at our house through the rear window as we drive away, rattling along the dirt road.

We weave deeper and deeper into the bush until I can't even see the house any more. We're silent in the car, as if the people might be able to hear us.

They'll be in the house now. I imagine them touching Mum's things and swallow. 'What did you do?' I ask Dad under my breath.

He's silent. I watch his profile. His jaw is tight.

Time crawls until Grandma quietly asks, 'Do you think they saw us?'

'I don't know. Just let me think,' he says, gripping the steering wheel.

I turn and focus behind us, searching for any signs we're being followed. All I can see is darkness.

After about twenty minutes we reach a main road and Dad switches on the headlights. We're joining the highway. There are no other cars in sight. He turns on to it and presses the accelerator. We speed up, getting further and further away from home.

'Who are they?' I ask. 'Why are we running away from them?'

He sighs. 'I borrowed some money from people I thought were my friends,' he says, finally. 'They want it back.'

'So, pay them,' I say.

'It's not that simple,' says Dad. 'They want more now.'

I check behind us again.

I'm still staring backwards at the dark road when Dad slams on the brakes and we're all thrown forward. I grip on to the seat. Grandma yelps as Polly falls on her. I turn forwards just in time to see the ute skidding towards a big grey object in the middle of the road. The car veers to the side as Dad spins the steering wheel. We slide closer and closer and I'm sure we're going to collide. This is it. I scrunch my eyes shut.

Not again. Please not again.

CHAPTER THREE
Crash

Grandma reaches for my shoulders and presses against me to break the impact. The car screeches to a halt in a cloud of dust.

My body jolts forward then back again as the seatbelt catches me.

For a moment we all just sit there. I know exactly what's flashing though our minds; images of Mum.

A sharp pain fills my head, not because I hurt it, but because of the memories filling it. I rub my palm against my forehead and wait for the wave of wooziness to pass.

'Everyone all right?' asks Dad, turning.

I nod but my ears ring and my fingers tingle. The second thing I've been scared of since Mum died is driving.

'Yes,' says Grandma, rubbing her chest.

'What is it?' I ask, peering at the mound in the middle of the road.

'A kangaroo,' says Dad. 'Someone must have hit the poor thing earlier.' He glances back at me.

'We should move it out of the way so no one else gets hurt,' I say.

Dad nods. 'Help me?'

Grandma opens the door and I drop to the tarmac, landing on shaky legs. The kangaroo is lit up by the headlights. It's still and dark blood coats its nose. Flies rest on the corners of its open eyes. I want to close them.

I walk towards the kangaroo, place my hand on its chest and feel its rough, bristly hair. There's no breath. No heartbeat. No life.

I slide my palm down its side and the kangaroo's skin gets warmer. I press gently on its stomach and feel the tiny pulse of a heart, beating too fast.

'It's still alive!' I shout.

Dad races over and kneels next to me.

'No – it's too late for the mum,' he says. 'But look . . .' He pulls the kangaroo's pouch open. A rush of heat hits my face along with the smell of sour milk. A baby joey stares up at us through big eyelashes. Its pointy ears look too big for its head. I reach down and it breathes through its nostrils on to my hand.

'Luckily it's big enough to have fur,' says Dad. 'It should survive out of the pouch.'

'Let me see,' says Grandma, kneeling next to us.

'We can't leave it here,' I say, softly. 'Please, Dad?'

Dad hesitates and glances around us. 'We'll find an animal centre on the way,' he replies. Dad tries not to show it, but he loves animals as much as I do.

He rummages in the car and returns with a knife from his outback emergency box and an emptied tote bag. Kneeling beside the kangaroo, he says, 'I'm going to have to cut the pouch to get it out.'

Grandma reaches for my hand as Dad carefully pierces the skin around the pouch, slicing through the flesh until it's separated from the mother kangaroo.

I wince. *Please be okay, please be okay* repeats in my head.

Dad leaves the joey suckling on the teat and cuts that off from the mother too.

Dad slides the joey into the bag. She's about a foot long, with an equally long tail. Blood stains the material a dark red. Grandma tucks the bag under her clothes to keep the joey warm with her body heat. She secures it using her shawl as a sling. When she pulls her coat closed at the front, you wouldn't even know there was a joey inside.

Dad glances around us again. 'We need to get out of here,' he says.

We drag the kangaroo to the side of the road before squeezing into the ute and setting off again.

'Can I hold her?' I ask.

Grandma shakes her head. 'Not yet. We need to keep the little one as calm as possible.'

Polly sniffs Grandma's coat.

'Lie down,' I say, commanding Polly to stay by my feet, even though she'd never hurt anything.

'We'll find a vet or someone to take her when we reach Perth,' says Dad.

We drive all night through the Great Sandy Desert on long roads that stretch for miles.

'You should take a break,' says Grandma to Dad eventually. 'Get some sleep. We're far away now. They won't find us.'

He sighs and nods, and we pull over on to the side of the road. I try to stay awake.

The third thing I've been afraid of since Mum died is going to sleep. I'm scared I'll never wake up again. Usually, I stay up and read until I'm so exhausted I can't help falling asleep, but I don't have my book now. I sing songs quietly to myself instead.

In the end, tiredness takes over and I drift in and out of sleep until the sun is up and we're driving again, going through red sands under a deep blue sky. We pass giant termite mounds and huge rocks made from layers of sandstone, each layer a different shade of orange. The air above the tarmac road shimmers from the heat.

Dad passes me a strip of paper. I stare at it.

Three tickets for a cruise.

'We're travelling by boat?' I ask, startled.

I thought it would be fun to try something different,' he says with a brief grin. 'It will be nicer for Polly to travel this way too.'

Grandma leans over to me. 'I think Dad's being kind to his old mum.'

I'd forgotten that Grandma's scared of flying.

I stare at the tickets in my hand. I've never been on a boat before in my life.

I look at Dad's strained face and wonder what else he's hiding.

CHAPTER FOUR

Ship

After several hours, the landscape becomes more urban and soon we enter a city.

Grandma peeks at the joey under her coat and smiles at me. 'She's sleeping.'

My stomach twinges as I recognise the buildings and criss-crossing roads outside.

Perth.

It was where we had Mum's funeral.

She died on a Friday, the same day the roses bloomed. She'd been watching and waiting for them to open every day.

'Mum didn't get to see them,' I had said.

'Maybe they came out to say goodbye,' Grandma had replied.

I picked them before the funeral and scattered them over her coffin.

'Ruby.' Dad's voice snaps me out of the memories. 'Can you keep an eye out for vets?'

I scan the buildings we pass. Grandma checks under her coat again. 'I think she's a fighter.'

'There!' I say and point at a small building with VETERINARY CLINIC written in blue letters on the outside.

'Good luck, little one,' I whisper as Grandma disappears inside.

We wait for what feels like for ever. Dad glances in the rear-view mirror at the cars passing us.

'We're going to India to get away from the people who came to our house, aren't we?' I say.

He's quiet.

'Do you even have a job there?' I continue.

'I do have a job, I promise. And I'll sort this all out, Ruby.' He turns in the chair and smiles at me. It doesn't make me feel better. 'A new start. It will be good for all of us.'

I turn away from him and rest my head against the window. I don't want a new start. I just want things to go back to the way they were before Mum died.

'What's going on in there?' mutters Dad, nodding towards the vets. He drums his fingers against the steering wheel.

Grandma returns. She's clutching a carrier bag by her side.

'I bought a snack,' she says quickly, seeing us looking at the bag.

'From the vets? They have food on the boat,' replies Dad.

Polly barks at her as she gets into the car, sniffing her coat.

Grandma nudges Polly away.

'Will the joey be okay?' I ask.

'They said she's big enough to be out of any real danger. She simply needs a carer.'

I breathe a sigh of relief.

We continue until we reach Freemantle and the ocean. Skyscrapers and cranes rise into the skyline. The cruise ship towers out of the water, bigger than the other boats bobbing by its side. It gleams in the sunlight.

'We can board,' says Dad, pointing at a queue of people gathered on the ramp.

He unpacks the car before kneeling and hiding the keys on top of the back tyre.

'I've arranged for someone to collect the ute,' he explains.

'When are we coming back?' I ask.

'Someday,' he says, straightening and standing. 'Someday.'

We stand on the top deck together as the ship pulls away from Australia. Polly is by my side. A salty breeze whips my long hair across my face.

Dad's tense body seems to relax as he leans against the rail next to me, but all I feel is sadness to be leaving. I didn't get to say goodbye to Emily and my friends or even the house. I think of all Mum's belongings that we left behind. My stomach turns as I realise I forgot her favourite orange scarf. It was the one thing that still held her citrusy scent.

Last time I was here, we scattered Mum's ashes along the beaches hugging the mainland. The wind picked them up and carried some out to the ocean.

I wonder if they fell on the water below me.

'Follow me, Mum,' I whisper into the wind and clutch my necklace. 'I don't want to leave you behind.'

I wake up the next morning, and for a moment I lie there, wanting to believe that the past day didn't happen. I'm lying on a top bunk in a cabin with portholes. The boat rocks underneath me. I groan, sit up and swing my legs over the side.

'Grandma?'

Silence.

I scan the room: my clothes are still in a pile on the floor; Grandma's suitcase is in the corner; everything's the same as last night. Climbing down the ladder, I see Grandma's bed is made. Polly's gone too.

The rooms in the cabin are arranged in a line, each with doors connecting to a hallway between them and a shared bathroom. I tiptoe past the bathroom and into Dad's. There's a note on the table. I rush towards it.

Gone to breakfast — see you there. Didn't want to wake you.

I dress quickly and hurry to the restaurant. I spot Dad and Grandma, huddled in a corner with a table full of toast and fruit.

Dad waves at me.

I feel a rush of anger at him for acting as if nothing's happened and pull my chair close to Grandma's, sitting as far away from him as possible.

'I have a surprise for you,' says Dad, passing me a bowl of fruit. 'One of my new bosses used to work at a wildlife sanctuary. He said he'd be delighted to teach you about the animals around the hotel. Think of the photographs you could take.'

I shrug.

Grandma's canvas shoulder bag hangs off the chair. The fabric gathers and stretches as if something is wriggling inside.

I jump and narrow my eyes. Two grey furry ears poke out the top.

My mouth drops open. Grandma raises her finger to her lips.

'I need to go for a rest,' she says to Dad.

'I'll walk back with you,' I say and grab some toast to take with me.

'What happened?' I ask, once we're out of earshot.

'They wouldn't take her at the vets,' whispers

Grandma. 'They had no room. I panicked. I couldn't leave the poor thing to die.'

'She needs a proper carer,' I say, opening Grandma's bag and staring down at the baby kangaroo's big eyes and nose. I kneel to look closer. The roo reaches her head out and kisses my nose with hers. It's soft and warm. My heart melts.

'I know how to take care of a kangaroo, Ruby,' says Grandma. 'Make a pouch. Keep her warm. Feed her kangaroo milk. The people next door raised one, remember?'

'But not on a cruise ship! And not in India.'

The roo flicks one ear.

Grandma raises her eyebrows at me.

'Being a carer is a full-time job,' I add. Mum always taught me that nature must be respected and that cute baby animals can grow up to be huge and wild. They aren't pets.

When we reach our cabin, Grandma lifts a pillowcase pouch out of her shoulder bag with the kangaroo inside. She hangs it on a coat hook, off the ground.

'I've named her Joey,' says Grandma, unscrewing a tub of powder with a picture of a kangaroo and a koala on the front. She pulls out a baby bottle with an extra-long teat. 'They gave me this to feed her at the vets. I've got enough to last until she's weaned.'

'How are we going to keep this a secret from Dad?'

'I don't know, but he can't find out. All it would do is cause him unnecessary worry.'

'At least he chose the front room. He shouldn't have to come in here very often,' I reply.

I stroke Joey's soft nose and she rests her head against the pillowcase and closes her eyes. Polly curls up next to the pouch on top of my feet, looking up at us.

'I can't believe you smuggled a kangaroo out of Australia, Grandma,' I whisper, shaking my head.

CHAPTER FIVE

Sea

On our second day at sea, Dad joins me and Grandma on the open-air terrace at the bow of the ship. He leans against the guardrail, watching the waves below.

'Dad,' I say quietly. 'How did it happen? How did those people end up at our house?'

'It was only one person to begin with,' says Dad, after a pause. 'Until the payments weren't enough.'

'Why didn't you tell the police?' I ask.

'They're dangerous people. I was frightened they'd hurt you or Grandma.'

Grandma rests a hand on his shoulder.

I remember the headlights coming up the driveway, my bedroom, and everything we left behind.

'I really am sorry, darling,' Dad says, turning to face me. 'What can I do to make the move better?'

My chest tightens. He made us flee in the middle of the night, leave behind Mum's belongings, move across the ocean, and he thinks he can make it better?

'You don't get it.' I lift my head and gaze out to the ocean. Sunlight dances on the rippling surface.

'Then tell me,' he replies.

'There's nothing you can do!' I say, my voice rising. A few bystanders shuffle away. 'I don't have any friends in India. I don't even have any memories of Mum there.'

Dad breathes in sharply and clasps his hands together. 'I know. But I met your mum in India. She's every bit there as she is here. In a way, you're following in her footsteps.'

I shrug but something inside me softens slightly.

'She'll always be with you wherever you go,' adds Grandma. 'Remember that.'

I nod but just in case, later that day, I decide to write her a note. I know it's a weird thing to do but it makes me feel better. I dot the Is with stars like she used to.

Mum. We're moving to India. You've been there before so you know where it is. I don't know the exact location yet, except that it's on top of a mountain. See you there. Love, Ruby.

I rip it up and scatter it into the waves below, imagining them floating down to her. The pieces flutter down to the water, resting on the surface before sinking. Some are whipped up by the wind and disappear into the sky.

That evening Grandma and I return to our room to discover Joey's learnt how to jump out of the pillowcase pouch and hop about the room. She's as tall as my knees and her feet are as long as her legs. She leaps up to me and sniffs my hands before losing her balance and toppling over. She's been chewing on Grandma's shoe which is soaked and tattered.

Dad knocks on the door.

I spin my head round to look at Grandma, eyes wide.

'Get her in the bathroom,' Grandma says, passing me a bottle.

She opens the door to Dad as I close the one to the bathroom.

Muffled voices filter through. Joey squeaks at the sight of the bottle.

'What was that?' I hear Dad ask from the cabin.

'Ruby's in the bathroom,' says Grandma.

Joey sucks on the bottle noisily before leaping out of the pillowcase and into my arms, knocking me into the towel rail.

'What's going on in there?' asks Dad, tapping on the bathroom door. 'Are you all right, Ruby?'

'I'm fine.' I flush the toilet to cover the noise. 'Just feeling a bit seasick,' I shout through the door.

'Can I get anything to make you feel better?'

'No, thanks.'

I gather Joey's pillowcase pouch in my arms to keep her still. She rests her nose on my shoulder, tired from her playful burst.

Grandma opens the door a few minutes later. 'That,' she says, 'was far too close.'

I nod and wish Mum was here. She would have loved Joey.

Imagining Mum with Joey makes my chest feel tight. For a long time, it was too hard to think about her at all. I'd picture her as clearly as if she was next to me – her smile and chipped front tooth, the lemon eucalyptus scent she wore as mosquito repellent – but it would just remind me of everything I'd lost, so I stopped picturing her at all. Now I can almost see her again, stroking Joey's soft little nose, and my heart aches. I think of my letter bobbing around on the waves. I wonder whether, in some way, it will reach her.

CHAPTER SIX

Equator

After six days on the cruise through the Indian Ocean, Dad hammers on my door.

'Come quickly,' he says. 'We're crossing the equator!'

Polly and Joey are curled up in a ball together by my feet at the end of the bed, hidden under a blanket. I wriggle my toes out from beneath them.

I go on to the deck and join Grandma and the other passengers leaning over the rails and staring into the deep blue water.

'How do we know when we cross it?' I ask Dad.

I was half expecting there to be an actual line drawn across the ocean.

'I'm not sure,' replies Dad.

'Now!' shouts someone at the back of the crowd and everyone cheers.

'At this moment we're exactly halfway between the North Pole and the South Pole,' says Grandma.

White foaming waves gather where the hull meets the water.

'In the middle of the earth,' I say. Although all I can see is ocean. I take a photo anyway, a seagull flying into the shot just as the shutter clicks.

'Did you miss India when you first came to Australia?' I ask Grandma.

'Every day,' she says, putting her arm over my shoulder and squeezing it. 'But it got easier with time. There were lots of new things to keep me entertained. I'd never seen the sea before I came to Australia.'

'Never?'

'I grew up inland.'

'What did you think?' I ask her.

'That it stretched further than I ever could have imagined. And that I couldn't wait to dive into it even though I didn't know how to swim.'

I smile.

'Did you know that it was me who gave you your middle name?' she asks.

I shake my head no. My middle name is Sky — unusual, but I never questioned where it came from.

'I wanted you to remember that wherever you are in the world, you'll always be under the same sky as the people that love you.'

I smile.

Sunlight catches the flecks of grey in Dad's dark hair and trimmed beard. As we walk down the stairs back to the cabin I remember how he stopped caring about his appearance after Mum died. For months his hair was long and tangled and his beard thick and full.

Inside Dad's room, I open the door to the hallway leading to my bedroom and Joey hops straight past me.

'Wait,' I say and lunge to grab her. I must have

left our bedroom door open as I rushed on to the deck earlier.

I glance up to see Dad's mouth fall open as Joey hops in circles around him. With each bounce, she springs herself upwards, getting faster and faster, her large eyes shining.

'That's not ours,' says Dad. There's a pause while he looks slowly round at us. 'Is it?'

Joey spots me and bounds to my feet. Dad glances at the main door and ushers us into my bedroom, slamming the sliding doors shut behind him. He turns to glare at us.

I grab the pillowcase off the hook and Joey leaps inside, headfirst. She readjusts, sticks her head out and licks her own nose.

Grandma and I sit on the bed. I swing my legs and Polly lies across Grandma's lap.

'She's called Joey,' I say, finally.

'I don't care,' says Dad, pacing back and forth. 'It's not coming with us.'

'Please?' I ask.

'What were you thinking, Mum?' he asks. 'I thought you knew better. You've jeopardised our whole move. Who knows how many laws we've broken.'

'I can pretend it's another dog,' Grandma says.

'We're sorry,' I say. 'Please Dad, just this once. Can we keep her?'

Joey leaps out of the pillowcase, bounces towards him and licks his fingers. He pulls them away from her and she starts sucking on his shirt instead. Polly cocks her head and looks at Dad. She whines as if she wants Joey to stay with us too.

Dad storms out of the cabin.

'What do you think will happen now?' I ask Grandma, mixing Joey's milk in the bottle.

'I don't know, dear.'

But I know what we're both thinking. If Dad tells anyone about Joey, they'll take her away.

CHAPTER SEVEN

Kangaroo

That night I dream the moneylenders surround the ship with deafening motor boats and break in. They surge on board, trampling our belongings and dragging Dad, Grandma, Polly and Joey away. Suddenly the scenery changes and I'm all alone on top of a snowy mountain. I wake sweating and out of breath. Through the darkness I hear the comforting rumble of Grandma's snore below me. Then I pick out Polly's lighter breathing, almost a whistle. I have to lean over the side of the bed to check on Joey. I see the familiar lump in the pillow case and know she's there.

I won't have any chance of getting back to sleep unless I know Dad's still there too. I switch on my keychain torch and climb down the ladder. It gently creaks. Along the corridor, I ease the door to his cabin open and tiptoe towards the bed, but halfway across the room I bump into a chest of drawers. A glass tips and crashes to the floor, splashing my toes with water. I jump. Polly barks from my room.

'Who's there?' Dad shouts, leaping out of bed.

'It's me,' I say. My voice sounds very small. He switches on a light.

'What are you doing sneaking around, Ruby? Haven't you got us in enough trouble with that kangaroo?'

I try to tell him about my dream, but the words

don't come. I stare at my hands instead.

He sees my face drop. 'I'm sorry,' he says. 'I didn't mean that.'

'What's all this noise about?' asks Grandma, bustling in. She stops when she sees me. 'What are you doing awake, Ruby?' Joey bounces in behind her.

I don't know what to say so I stay quiet and kneel to stroke Joey's chin.

'You were probably worrying about Joey,' Grandma says and looks searchingly towards Dad.

Dad shakes his head. 'We can't keep it. I'm sorry. The last thing this family needs is more drama.'

They both turn to look at me and Joey, who bounces on to my knee and lies across my lap.

'Maybe a joey is exactly what this family needs,' says Grandma.

Dad presses his fingers against his forehead. He gazes between us.

Joey nuzzles into my arms and I hug her close to me.

Dad's expression softens. 'I can't believe I'm saying this but fine. If you make it to India without anyone finding out, you can keep it.'

'Really?' asks Grandma.

'But you two are taking full responsibility for it, all right?'

'Thanks, Dad,' I say, standing with Joey.

He puts his arm around me and squeezes my shoulder. 'We can take shifts to make sure it stays hidden. Luckily we only have one more day.'

Grandma nods.

'Deal,' I say.

I hardly leave the cabin the next day, and spend hours playing with Joey and watching over her.

'We're arriving in India soon,' says Grandma, bringing me a sandwich in the evening.

She packs the last of her clothes in her suitcase while I eat.

Joey's fast asleep and one of her ears pokes out the top of the pillowcase and flicks back and forth.

A while later Dad rushes in. 'I want you to see this,' he says, grabbing my hand and leading me up to the deck as we pull into the dock. He leaps up the stairs two at a time. 'Look,' he whispers.

It must be the middle of the night, but the city is awake below us in a sea of lights. I've never seen so many. Anticipation flutters in my chest.

As we get closer, streetlights illuminate a market bustling with people and cars. Flickering fires dot the sides of the roads. The air is humid, unlike the dry desert I'm used to. Polly follows us on to the deck and sniffs the air.

Later, as we disembark, we have to queue to pass through X-rays and metal detectors. It's chaotic and people bump into each other to get in line. I stay close to Grandma and Dad. Police stand guard with guns tucked under their arms.

I pause before the exit and cling to the rail with one hand. The air is sticky and I feel dizzy from the height. I push away thoughts of Joey being found and Grandma going to prison.

'You okay?' Dad asks, turning.

I nod and step after him.

I notice Grandma has taken off her jewellery. We all ignore the bag on the inside of Grandma's coat holding Joey. I hope she doesn't wriggle too much. Polly waits patiently by my side. After Grandma places her suitcase on the X-ray, she leaves her coat on and walks through the metal detector. I wait with Dad. My breaths are quick and loud.

The machine doesn't beep and the security guards wave her through.

She did it.

We follow her and collect our bags from the conveyer strip together. Grandma takes my hand and squeezes it.

'Stop,' says an officer.

My heart leaps.

'You didn't take off your coat,' he says to Grandma.

'But I've already been through,' she says.

He points back towards the conveyer, blocking her way.

'Is this really necessary?' asks Dad.

The officer nods sternly.

Grandma rests her suitcase by her feet and unbuttons her coat.

Joey's underneath. Adrenaline races through my chest.

Grandma slides off the coat and the bag containing Joey at the same time. She gently drops the Joey bag next to the pile of suitcases on the ground.

I glance at the officer. He hasn't noticed the bag.

'I'll look after your luggage while you go back,' I say, rushing forward and scooping up the bag with Joey.

Dad steps in front of me and unzips a suitcase, pretending to search for something, blocking me from sight.

Grandma hands the officer her coat. 'There you go.'

They walk back and he places it on the conveyer and asks her to step through the X-ray again.

Polly stands guard next to me and Joey, as if

she can tell we need protecting.

The officer waves Grandma past and she joins us.

'Welcome to India,' says Dad, proudly.

We step on to land with a border collie, a joey kangaroo and a taxidermy python, and my insides are yelling with delight that we all made it.

'This way to the train station,' says Dad, pointing.

We follow him into the bustling market, rolling our suitcases behind us and weaving around rickshaws and motorbikes. We pass stalls selling colourful bangles, bindis and shawls. Stainless steel pots and pans clink as a man unhooks a pressure cooker for a customer next to us. A cow lies in the road, swishing his head back and forth to avoid the flies. The smell of fried bread wafts over the crowd and I spot oily *parathas* cooking at the side of the road. Chatter fills the air. A girl with short hair and yellow sandals passes me and smiles and I feel a twinge of excitement. Perhaps making new friends here won't be as hard as I thought.

A tree, at the edge of the line of shops, twinkles with fireflies and I stop and stare.

'Will you look at that,' says Dad in awe.

Grandma beckons for my camera and gestures at me and Dad to stand together.

'Smile,' she says.

And for the first time in a while, I do.

CHAPTER EIGHT

India

I catch my first glimpse of the Himalayas the next day as we turn a corner in the taxi. After an overnight train journey and a bus ride, we're leaving the plains of the Punjab and climbing into the winding pine-covered foothills of Himachal Pradesh. The mountains span across the horizon, jagged and snow tipped. I can't take my eyes off them.

We get higher and higher, driving around hairpin bends until the driver stops in a small town. Buildings, several stories high, line the main road. Red monkeys chase each other along balcony rails and people sip chai in the cafés.

'This is as far as I can go,' says the taxi driver, stopping in front of a fruit shop overflowing with hanging bananas and baskets of papayas and limes.

Dad's glancing at the map in his hand. 'It's a bit further, isn't it? There's a road that curves slightly to the left. I think it's that one.' He points to the left fork in the road.

The taxi driver opens his door.

'But it's at least another ten-minute drive,' says Dad. 'On the map it looks like you can keep going.'

'Sorry,' the driver shakes his head apologetically. He closes the door, opens the boot and unloads our suitcases. 'You'll have to get someone else to take you the rest of the way.'

We stand at the side of the road with our luggage and watch the driver pull away.

The air is crisp and clear.

'I bet the road gets worse,' says Dad. 'He probably doesn't want to scratch his car.'

Grandma nods in agreement.

We stand outside a dry food store, next to baskets of spices. I recognise the bright yellow turmeric, dried chilies and the scent of cinnamon.

Two rickshaws fly past and Dad waves them both down. 'Durga mountain,' he says.

A strained look appears on the first driver's face and he shakes his head at the words before the rickshaw rattles away. The second driver purses his lips and follows.

'Wait,' shouts Dad after them, arms in the air.

'Are we going to have to walk?' I ask.

'Let's ask in the shop, darling,' Grandma says to Dad.

Inside, I gaze at the shelves of biscuits hungrily.

'Why do you want to go there?' asks the owner, filling a sack with dried kidney beans.

'I'm managing the new hotel there.'

He eyes us warily. 'You won't find anyone willing to go up there but you can hire my donkeys to carry your bags.'

'Thanks,' says Dad. Relief flashes across his face.

'You're not coming with us?' asks Grandma.

'I have to look after the shop. Bring the donkeys back when you're done.'

Outside, he fastens the suitcases to the harnesses on two donkeys.

'Follow the road,' he says. 'Take a left at the top and continue on the footpath. You can't miss it.'

The donkeys' hooves clop on the tarmac. We wind up through thick pine forest, leaving the town far below us until we're surrounded only by trees, high in the foothills of the Himalayas.

Polly runs up and down panting, thankful to stretch her legs. I'm carrying Joey and she pokes her head out of the pouch and sniffs the air, her nose wrinkling.

I catch glimpses of a building through the trees.

'Is that it?' I ask, jogging ahead.

'Must be,' Dad shouts after me.

The building comes into view and my stomach drops. I wasn't expecting this. The hotel is an abandoned two-story building with boarded up windows and a rusty blue tin roof. It's surrounded by a chest-high wall covered in overgrown climbers and weeds.

A boy in a long coat sits on the wall wearing a rigid woollen hat with a flat top and vertical stripes across the front of it in earthy colours.

He stands when he sees me. We meet eyes, his are deep and dark. He's almost as tall as Dad. Probably a year or two older than me.

A big mountain dog with a fluffy tail waits by his side.

Polly rushes forward to his dog.

'Come back,' I call, but they're already sniffing each other, tails wagging.

'Praveen, right?' says Dad, catching up to me and approaching the boy. He shakes his hand. 'We're leasing the hotel from Praveen's father,' he explains to me.

'Hi,' says Praveen. 'My father apologises he can't be here but he asked me to show you the place.'

'Is this it?' I ask, staring at the dishevelled building.

Dad nods.

'I expected it to be more . . .' Grandma searches for the right words. 'Ready for guests.'

'We'll have it up and running in no time,' says Dad, but I hear his voice waiver.

Something moves in Praveen's front coat pocket and I look closer: two baby goats snuggle inside giant pockets on his chest. Their tiny heads poke out of the top with pink noses and floppy ears. One makes a high mewing sound.

'Are these your goats?' I ask.

'Yes,' he replies.

I reach forwards to stroke one.

'Hands off. You might scare them.'

I stop, taken aback.

Dad pushes the stiff gate open.

I hop on to the wall, pausing at the top and sighing. We really are in the middle of nowhere. Thick jungle and tall pine trees surround us on all sides and beyond it rise mountains and snowy peaks.

Grandma leads in the donkeys with our luggage and Joey.

We walk through the neglected garden, overgrown with giant daisies, purple orchids and orange lilies.

Joey squirms in the pillowcase and I stop to adjust her. My arms ache.

'What's in there?' asks Praveen.

'Nothing,' I reply.

'Is it a goat?'

'No, it's a kangaroo,' I say.

'I've never seen a kangaroo,' says Praveen, eyes widening and stepping towards it.

'Hands off,' I reply, mimicking him. 'You might scare her.'

Praveen laughs. 'Fair enough.'

He looks at me for a minute, then lifts one of the new-born goats out of his pockets. It's the size of a small chihuahua.

'They're twins,' he says. 'Be careful. They were

premature and aren't feeding properly.'

I stroke its soft fur. It bleats and licks my finger with its long tongue before nibbling my hand. It tickles.

'How long since someone lived here?' Dad asks Praveen.

He shrugs. 'A long time. We inherited it from my Great Grandpa before I was born but we've never lived here – we have a house down in the village. My whole family lives there and my parents didn't want to be far away from them.'

'So it's just been sitting here, empty for years?' I ask.

He nods and unlocks the padlock on the front door, stepping aside to let us enter.

I blink, my eyes adjusting to the darkness of the hall after the brightness outside. Praveen breaks the wooden boards off the windows so the light can get in.

Dad opens his arms. 'Welcome to your new home, the soon-to-be Mountain View Hotel.'

I roll my eyes.

We walk through to a big room with a table and chairs, curtains and a giant fireplace. Everything is coated in a thick layer of dust. I can't even see the pattern on the tattered rug on the floor.

I open the curtains and moths fly at me. I sneeze; it smells of mildew. Dead flies lie in piles on the window sills, coated in spider webs.

'Nothing a lick of paint can't fix,' says Grandma bravely, heading off to explore.

Dad nods and runs his hand through his hair. I search for a light switch but don't find one. Cracks run down the stone walls.

'Ruby, come up here!' says Grandma, from upstairs. 'This can be your bedroom. We can decorate it however you want. I'll take the one next to it.'

There are eight bedrooms upstairs, three downstairs, and a big living area and kitchen and three bathrooms. The only room that looks like it has had people in it recently is the kitchen. There are food wrappers and a torch on the side.

'Who's been in the kitchen?' I ask.

'Mr Bhat and Mr Anand come here sometimes,' says Praveen.

'Who are they?' I ask.

'My hotel bosses,' says Dad.

'Where are the lights?' I ask. 'And the sockets?'

'There's no electricity,' says Dad. 'Yet.'

'Seriously?' I ask, shivering. I make a mental note to place a torch in every room. It takes preparation to hide from the dark.

It's no better in the bathroom; when I turn the tap above the sink it makes a glugging sound but nothing comes out.

'Where's the water tank?' Dad asks Praveen.

The water tank turns out to be a swimming

pool sized pond in the garden full of murky green water. Dragonflies skim the surface.

'That explains all the buckets in the bathroom,' says Grandma.

'There's no way I'm showering in that,' I say, pointing at the water.

'Don't worry, Ruby,' says Dad. 'I'll go down to the village and rustle up some help tomorrow.'

I remember the looks on people's faces when we told them we were going to Durga mountain. I get the feeling no one wants to come up here. I can see why: there's nothing here but this wreck of a building.

Grandma soon discovers a cupboard with a hard broom and we spend the afternoon sweeping and cleaning. Praveen disappears and returns with bundles of wood and kindling. Then he climbs on to the roof and pokes sticks down the chimney to check for bird's nests.

'It'll get cold tonight,' he says. 'You'll want a fire.'

When he's done he harnesses the donkeys. 'I'll take these back to town for you.'

Outside, pine cones from the cedar trees crunch under my feet. Polly and his dog bark and chase after each other.

'What's your dog called?' I ask.

'Kuttani,' he replies.

'Wait,' says Dad, rushing out from behind

me. 'I forgot to ask where the drinking water is.'

Praveen pauses by the gate. 'The spring is over there,' Praveen says, pointing to the path on my right. 'And beyond it is the lower path to my village.' He points again, this time to the path on my left. 'Down there is bear rock. It's a giant boulder that sticks out from the slope. Don't ever go there,' he says seriously. 'It's where the bears live.'

A loud rumbling echoes off the peaks in the distance. I watch as a cascade of rocks slides down a tall mountain. Only a few trees dot its rocky terrain. A cloud floats in front.

Praveen follows my gaze. 'And up there is snow leopard territory,' he adds.

I look up at the jagged peak and feel a shiver of excitement.

CHAPTER NINE

Scorpion

As it gets dark, Dad places the kindling in the fireplace with the bigger logs on the top.

'See if you can find some matches in the kitchen,' he says.

I open drawers and spot a rusty tin, which rattles when I pick it up. There's a pattern engraved on the outside which I trace with my finger. I lift the lid off. Inside is a pile of what look like teeth.

'Dad!' I shout, dropping the tin. Some of the teeth scatter on to the floor. They're curved and pointed.

Not teeth, but claws.

There must be at least fifty of them.

Dad rushes in as I'm peering at them more closely.

'Look at this,' I say. 'What kind of claws are they?'

'I don't know. They look like they've been there for a hundred years,' he says, gathering them up with his hands and dropping them back into the tin. 'Where were they?'

I point to the drawer.

'Come on,' he says, putting them back and firmly shutting the drawer, 'I found some matches on the mantelpiece.'

As I turn something catches my eye outside.

'Look,' I say, tugging Dad's arm.

A green-tinted light shines through the trees

in the distance. It bobs up and down, as if it's moving by itself.

Dad checks the front door and bolts it tightly shut. 'It's just a shepherd,' he says.

But there's something about the way the light moves that gives me the creeps. A bird makes a call that sounds like 'toot toot' in the distance. It echoes off the hills around us.

Back in the living room Dad trickles kerosene on the logs and drops a lit match. The fire burns bright for a few seconds before calming down.

We pull our chairs close and soak up the heat. Polly lies on my feet, Joey in my arms.

'We'll sleep in here tonight,' says Dad.

Shadows dance against the stone mantelpiece.

That's when I notice something crawling over the fireplace.

Thick black bodies with curled tails and stingers on the ends. They appear from the cracks in the stones and are lit up by the light of the flames. Scorpions. Heading away from the fire. In seconds they're all over the place. On the wall, the bottom of the fireplace and around sleeping Polly's head on the floor.

I jump on top of the chair with Joey in my arms while Dad runs into the kitchen and returns with a brush and pan. Dad sweeps the scorpions up and drops them out the back door. Some are as long as my palm.

'They're not deadly or anything,' says Grandma, who has come to see what the commotion is about. 'But they'll give you a nice sting if they feel threatened.' She takes a pair of tweezers from her bag and gently picks up the scorpions around Polly one by one, lifting them by their stingers. 'Coming through,' she says as she dangles one in the air on her way out.

I lay a twig beside a smallish scorpion, hoping it will crawl on to the bark, so I can move it to the veranda, but it freezes and raises its stinger at the stick. I look around; most of the scorpions have already hidden. I imagine them lurking under my pillow and shiver.

'Well,' says Dad, checking his chair before sitting back down. 'Maybe we should sleep in the other room after all.'

'There are flies everywhere, and the other rooms smell like mould,' I reply. 'I'd rather sleep outside.'

'No way,' says Dad, crossing his arms. 'There are bears out there.'

'Get stung by scorpions or eaten by bears. Great choice. Thanks, Dad.'

His face crumples for a moment and I feel a twinge of guilt. But only for a second. It was his stupid choice to bring us here.

'I wish I had my tent,' I say.

'You do,' says Dad. 'I packed it for you.'

I stand and rummage through our luggage for my tent. I remember when Mum bought it for me two years ago for my birthday, after I told her I wanted to be a wildlife photographer when I grew up.

'Are you sure?' she had asked. 'You'll have to sit in a hide for days on end, waiting for an animal to appear.'

I finally find it and set it up at the back of the room, away from the fireplace. 'I'm sleeping in here from now on.'

'Do you need anything else, love?' asks Grandma, passing me Mum's quilt.

I shake my head; I don't feel like being around either her or Dad right now.

I crawl inside with a torch and curl up with Polly. Making sure there are no bugs inside, I zip the tent up, cutting myself off from it all and praying a scorpion doesn't crawl underneath and sting me through the sleeping mat.

I wrap the patchwork quilt around me. Mum hand stitched the pictures on to it when she was pregnant with me. She began with animals like elephants and tigers, but they turned out as grey rocks and orange dogs, so she moved on to moons, stars and clouds. Of the animals she tried stitching, only the snakes resembled themselves and even they looked a little bit like worms.

I switch on the torch and the tent glows yellow. The last time I was in this tent I was camping in our garden, trying to capture photos of nocturnal animals like echidnas. I remember the rustling of the Australian bush and later Mum's humming coming from the porch. It was the song she would sing me before we went to sleep. She had a beautiful voice, soft but clean pitched. I poked my head out to tell her she was scaring the animals away, but then I saw that she and Dad were dancing. Their outlines silhouetted as she twirled. So I took a photo of them instead.

I wonder if I'll ever be able to camp by myself again. The last time I did was before Mum went. Before I was afraid of the dark.

CHAPTER TEN

Spider

'Knock, knock,' says Dad, outside the tent.

For a second I don't know where I am. I open my eyes. Polly is pawing and whining at the entrance. I unzip the tent.

'Any bites or stings?' Dad asks, kneeling in the tent porch.

I shake my head and stretch. I feel as if I've been asleep for days.

'I made you a bottle for this one.' He passes me Joey's pouch.

'Thanks,' I reply, taking the bottle and tilting it towards Joey's mouth. She latches on and slurps the milk.

'I've been into town and got all the supplies we need,' he says excitedly. 'I even got you a present.' He passes me a book. The title says *Flora and Fauna of the Himalayas*. 'Grandma's been cleaning your bedroom. You can move in.'

'How long was I asleep for?' I ask, surprised he's done so much.

'Thirteen hours.' He smiles. 'I woke up early. Probably the jetlag.'

Later, I drag the tent up the stairs and groan when I reach the bedroom. It doesn't look any more exciting in daylight. A makeshift bed sits in the middle of an empty room with peeling white paint on the walls. The cement floor is cold under my feet. I glance out the window. There's nothing but trees outside. No other houses. No people.

Polly cocks her head to the side and places her paw on my shin. She always knows when I'm feeling bad.

'It's all going to be okay,' says Dad, carrying a suitcase with Grandma behind him.

I feel a twinge of irritation. 'Why do you keep saying that?' I ask.

'Because I believe it.'

'You shouldn't,' I snap. I can't help it. All of my misery and frustration and tangled up feelings explode. My words are like arrows directed at Dad. 'You told me our home in Australia would be okay. You told me Mum would be okay. Why do you think this is going to be any different?'

There's a silence that follows. He looks at the floor and sighs. 'I want you to know that I'm trying my best,' he says, gently. 'I hope you can believe that.' He places the new book on the bed and leaves.

I throw myself down on the makeshift bed.

Grandma sits next to me and thinks for a while. 'What about your camera?' she asks.

'What about it?' I reply, turning to look at her deep eyes.

'Could you pretend you're on a research trip for now, as if you've been sent to photograph as many species here as you can? Like your mum did with snakes. After a while it might not feel like you're pretending any more.'

I grunt back at her. She sighs, ruffles my hair, and leaves.

Grandma's right though. It's what Mum would do. She always made the best of things and I have to believe that even though I'm scared of things, I'm still a bit like her.

I sit up, and jump. On the wall beside me is a giant spider with furry legs. It's definitely a female. They're always bigger. I back away slowly. In Australia there were many venomous spiders. You have to be careful.

I reach for the book at the end of the bed. Flicking through the pages I stop on a picture that looks like the spider.

This house spider's bite isn't harmful to humans and they live for up to eight years.

I hold the book up and double check it's the same one.

'You can stay in my room,' I say to her. 'Just keep off the tent.'

She scuttles slowly into the corner as if in response and I give her a sharp nod. We have an agreement.

'I'll call you Georgina,' I say and take a photograph of her.

I wonder if Praveen knows more about the

spiders and wish he would come back and show me around. There's something about his smile and the way he cares for his goat kids that makes me want to see him again.

CHAPTER ELEVEN

Butterflies

I set off exploring after lunch. I remember the direction of bear rock and head the other way.

'You're coming with me,' I say to Polly, leaving Joey wrapped up with Grandma. At least there are no roads or cars up here; one less thing to be afraid of.

The earth smells different and doesn't have the copper tinge of the soil in Australia. I start on the path, stepping over vines, batting leaves out of my way. As I walk deeper into the jungle, the path gets thinner and thinner and then disappears completely. A bird flitters through the branches above me and I follow it down the hill until it flies out of sight. I stop and spin around. Everything looks the same. I don't even know which direction I came from. All I can see are tall trees and thick jungle.

I try to turn back but I don't know if I'm going the right way. My heart quickens as I race through the trees. Long hanging branches scratch my forehead.

Something rustles. I stop and Polly growls. Slightly below me a dark rock covered in moss juts out of the ground. My breath catches. *Bear rock*. Vines hang and swing around it. I crouch down and touch the top of it. The stone is cold. I'm standing in the places the sunlight doesn't reach.

Bears sleep in the daytime. It could be in its cave under the rock.

Twigs crack. My heart thuds.

'Stop,' hisses a voice.

I straighten and whip my head around like a scared meerkat, searching for the source of the voice. I spot Praveen, beckoning at me from higher up the slope.

'Get away from there,' he hisses, 'it's not safe.'

I clamber over the undergrowth towards him.

'I was looking for Kuttani,' he says. 'I didn't expect to find you here.'

'I got lost,' I whisper.

We creep round the side, giving the rock a wide berth, until we're back on a trail.

'Look,' says Praveen, pointing to the ground. There, in the dried mud, is a giant bear print.

'*Bhalu*,' he says. 'Bear.'

I nod.

'How do you know about the bear and all the things up here?' I ask once we're a safe distance away. 'Don't you live down in the village?'

'I'm a *Gaddi* shepherd,' he says proudly. 'I bring the goats up here to graze and stay with them every day. Once a year my dad and I go on a months-long trek over the mountains and let them graze along the way.'

'What about school?'

He shrugs. 'It's the holidays from May until

September. When school starts I'll do it before and after school. Dad's older now. He can't manage the walk like he used to.'

Polly and Kuttani bound into the undergrowth together, playing.

'Come back!' I yell after Polly. She's never usually this badly behaved.

She stops and barks before springing off into the jungle. I think about how I was feeling earlier, how this was the loneliest place I've ever been. I wonder whether Praveen ever feels the same.

'Doesn't it get boring being in the mountains the whole time by yourself?' I ask.

He smiles. 'I'm never by myself. Come, I'll show you.'

I follow Praveen as he winds in and out of the tall evergreen trees. Our footsteps thud against the ground. We trample on a bed of red petals from the rhododendron trees. They have dark gnarly wood that twists and turns and big matt leaves. Tiny hummingbirds and bees fly into the red tubular flowers, bunched together in a circle.

Praveen spots something on the ground. He bends and picks up a long black-and-white quill. 'The porcupine's been here,' he says, handing it to me. 'For you.'

I smile. 'Thanks.' I wrap my long hair around the quill and fasten it into a bun.

We pass a miniature white temple the size of a cardboard box. Praveen reaches in the open front and rings a bell. The clanging echoes across the valley.

'What is it?' I ask.

'My dad says the bell wards off evil, but my mum says it tells the gods that we're here and empties our thoughts in preparation for prayer.'

He dips his finger in a small bowl of red powder and draws a line on my forehead with it. His finger is warm. He draws one on himself too.

'That's Shiva's trident,' he says, seeing me eye the tridents stacked in the corner of the temple. 'The god of destruction and restoration.'

Praveen ducks under a vine and stops in front of a tree. The light casts dappled shadows and shimmering patterns on the floor.

'You have to promise not to tell anyone about this place,' he says.

'I promise,' I say. 'My lips are sealed.'

A clearing and a wooden building come into view. It's a large cabin with darkened windows and a thick padlock on the door.

'That's the boss's,' says Praveen, tilting his head towards the wooden building. He pats the trunk of a rhododendron tree next to it. 'But this is what I wanted to show you.'

The bark is knobbly and swirls into a pattern

of browns. Red petals from the last of the funnel shaped flowers cover the ground beneath the wide spread of branches and give off a faint sour smell.

'Can you climb?' continues Praveen, his gaze challenging. I nod. He jumps and catches the branches before pulling himself up.

'Here,' he says, offering a hand.

'I've got it,' I say, finding a dent to fit my toes in and stepping up on to the branch.

We climb and sit side by side. From here we can see out over everything – down into the valley and all the way to the snowy mountains in the distance. Rolling hills stretch below us. I notice specks of white being carried on the wind. They get closer. Wings. A kaleidoscope of butterflies flies up over our heads and off into the sky.

I've never seen so many.

'I told you I was never alone. It's their migration,' says Praveen, smiling at me. 'It happens every year. It's just started.'

As the butterflies surround me, I feel a little flutter of joy in my stomach. Something I haven't felt in a long time, since before Mum died.

I'd almost forgotten the feeling existed.

CHAPTER TWELVE
Tree

'It's magical!' I say, wondering how many other people have seen it.

'This was the first tree I ever climbed,' he says. There's a rustle above us. 'I'd like you to meet someone.' He makes a clicking noise with his tongue. A baby grey langur climbs down from the top branches. Its arms wrap around Praveen's neck before turning its head to look at me.

'Meet Bandar,' says Praveen, scratching the monkey's head with one finger.

'What are you? Some kind of animal whisperer?' I ask, secretly impressed.

Praveen laughs. 'She was stolen by a neighbouring troop, but she got away. I saw the whole thing. I'm hoping her mother will pass through again soon and collect her. In the meantime, I feed her every morning and most evenings.'

'Hi Bandar,' I say.

'It means monkey in Hindi,' he says.

'I wish I knew Hindi,' I say. 'Dad and Grandma never taught me.'

'I can teach you,' Praveen replies. 'If you want?'

I nod.

'Start with the names of animals, all right? You already know *bhalu*.'

'Bear,' I say. 'That one's easy. And now I know monkey – *bandar*.'

He looks towards the sun. It's already low in the sky.

'My cousin's looking after the goats today, but I have to help put them away for the night in the village. Want to help?'

I nod. 'I'd better tell Dad first.'

We climb down and start walking back to the hotel.

'Why does no one come up here?' I ask. 'Apart from you.'

'What do you mean?' he asks.

'The mountain. Why are people scared to come up here?'

'I don't know,' he says, but he looks at the ground as he says it.

'Look,' I say, stopping in the path and turning to him. 'Whatever it is, you can tell me. I can see you're not saying something and I'm sick of people keeping things from me.'

'Okay,' he says, startled by my outburst. 'If you must know, it's because the mountain is haunted by the Goddess Durga.'

I stare at him, taken aback by his matter of fact tone. 'Are you kidding? I don't believe in ghost stories like that.' It's true, I don't; if ghosts were real, then Mum would have haunted me by now.

'Well, this one's true,' he says calmly. 'The first people who came up here in 1905 tried to build a school. They cleared a big area of trees and the day after they'd finished there was a huge earthquake. They fled.'

'That doesn't prove anything,' I say. 'There are often earthquakes in mountains.'

'Legend has it the dad from the family that moved here afterwards followed the lights and fell off the cliff.'

'The green lights?' I ask. 'You've seen them?'

'Everyone's seen them,' replies Praveen. 'And last year, several people got attacked by a bear and then the next people to visit were hit by falling rocks.'

We walk in silence for a minute.

'Who's Durga?' I ask.

'Mother of the universe,' replies Praveen.

I pull my shawl closer around me and look around us, 'Do you believe in it?' I ask.

He nods.

'Has anything ever happened to you?' I ask.

'No,' he replies, shaking his head.

'Do you think I'll be okay?' I ask.

'I think you're safe as long as you treat the mountain with respect. I don't think Durga's angry. She's just like a mother protecting her child.'

'Ruby!' I hear Dad shouting my name as the hotel comes into sight. 'Ruby!'

'Dad?' I shout, quickening my pace. 'I'm here.'

He turns, sprints towards me and hugs me tight. 'Where have you been? I was so worried.' Grandma's behind him.

'I just went for a walk. Exploring.'

'You can't do that here. There are leopards and bears.'

'There were venomous snakes and spiders in Australia,' I reply.

'You can't go off by yourself, all right?'

'It's okay, Dad, I promise – I was with Praveen. I was going to ask if I could go to his house now . . .'

'Ruby,' he snaps. 'I've got enough to worry about right now with Mr Bhat on my back about getting the hotel up and running, okay?'

Praveen catches up to us.

'Hi,' he says, smiling. 'Is it okay if Ruby comes to my house? I said I'd show her the baby goats.'

There's a pause and then Dad nods, calmer now. 'You can go for an hour. I'll be there to collect you.'

I nod.

As I go to grab two big torches to take with me, I have an idea. 'Want to meet Joey before we go?' I ask Praveen.

He tilts his head to the side. 'Joey?'

'The kangaroo,' I say.

He grins. 'Definitely.'

Inside, we step over paint pots and brushes,

and around sheets covering the furniture. The door to the dining room is closed and inside Joey's doing bouncing laps around the table. Her long feet are almost the same length as her legs. She bounds towards us, using her muscular tail to balance.

Praveen beams at the sight of her and crouches to stroke the white blaze down her front. She rests her small front arms on his. I recognise the look of happiness on his face. I've never met anyone who's as obsessed with animals as I am. Even though I still miss Emily, I wonder whether – here on the other side of the world – I've found a friend.

CHAPTER THIRTEEN
Attack

The village is spread along a slope and has brightly coloured two or three story houses with balconies and slate roofs. Surrounding them are fields of wheat. The houses have paved courtyards where cows, sheep and goats are tethered. Hens dash past clucking. I smell sawdust and straw.

'Did I get you in trouble?' Praveen asks.

I guess he overheard Dad shouting at me. I shake my head. 'Dad's just worried about the hotel.' We wind between the houses on a narrow path, towards a stable at the edge of the village with a field behind it. I try and change the subject. 'Do you have any brothers and sisters?'

'I have two older brothers. One of my brothers is a paragliding instructor a few hours away, and the other is an engineer in—' He stops abruptly.

I follow his line of sight.

A boy about the same age as Praveen is storming towards us. A flock of goats gathers around the stable behind him.

'Amul?' shouts Praveen, quickening his pace to a run. 'What's wrong? What happened?'

I run after him.

'I lost another one,' says Amul angrily.

Praveen scans the flock with his eyes.

'It happened a minute ago as I was leading them back. I heard a rushing sound, turned my head, and Star was gone.'

It's not your fault.' Praveen places a hand on Amul's shoulder.

'I think it grabbed her from a tree.'

'A leopard attack,' says Praveen to me.

I gaze around at the thick forest in the distance. It's easy to forget that they're out there.

'We're losing one of the flock every week,' says Amul. 'There'll be no goats left at this rate.'

'That's not true,' replies Praveen, herding the rest of the goats and sheep into the stable.

'Where are the twin kids?' I ask. 'Are they okay?'

Amul points to a donkey nearby. I don't understand what I'm supposed to be looking at until I see a flash of movement and hear a bleat. The kids' heads poke out of pockets along the side of the donkey's saddle. I walk over and stroke their tiny heads and soft long ears while Praveen and Amul usher the last of the goats inside and bolt the stable door. There are two hand drums fastened on the donkey's saddle and I tap on the leather skin with one finger without thinking.

'Have you ever heard the *tabla* being played?' asks Amul, heading over.

I shake my head.

'Before you're even allowed to touch the instrument you have to be able to say the rhythm. Repeat after me. Ti-ra-ki-ta, Ti-ra-ki-ta.'

I repeat the syllables slowly.

'Is that the fastest you can say it?' asks Praveen.

'I've never heard of having to say tongue twisters in order to play the drums,' I reply and cross my arms.

He laughs.

'Listen and see if you can hear the same rhythm when I play the drums,' says Amul.

Amul flicks his wrist back and forth to press with the heel of his palm and tap with his fingers. He nods his head in time.

I sway to the rhythm and say the syllables under my breath along with the beats.

It feels like hardly any time has passed when Dad and Grandma stride up to us. 'Time to go, Ruby,' he says.

I nod. Pink wisps of cloud float above us and my stomach lurches suddenly. I was so caught up in the playing I didn't notice the time; unless we leave soon, we'll have to walk back through the forest in the dark.

'Watch out for your dog,' Amul says. 'They make perfect leopard snacks.'

I hold on to Polly tightly. I won't let her out of my sight from now on.

'I meant to tell you – it's Holi festival in the town next week,' says Praveen as we leave.

'What's Holi?' I ask, turning back.

'A celebration of spring,' says Dad. 'Mr Bhat and Mr Anand are arriving that morning and I want us all there to meet them, but you can go in the afternoon.'

'See you there,' says Praveen.

I wave, take a deep breath, and venture into the dark trees with Dad, Grandma and Polly.

'I know why no one will come up the mountain,' I say and I tell them about Durga and the earthquake, and the man who died following the green light.

'I don't know why people are so scared. It's only a legend,' I finish.

'Stories and words are powerful. Whispers become rumours and rumours become believed,' says Grandma.

I spot the green light in the distance. It stays still and illuminates the tops of the trees in an eerie green haze. 'There is something creepy about it,' I say slowly.

We stop and watch the light together.

'I told you, it's a shepherd,' says Dad.

But I don't think I believe him.

CHAPTER FOURTEEN

Bosses

Over the next week the house is a rush of activity as we prepare for Mr Bhat and Mr Anand's visit.

'They told me I could manage the hotel as if it were my own. I simply have to have it up and running within a few weeks,' says Dad, at breakfast. 'They're trusting me with a lot. Let's show them what we can do.'

Together, we paint the walls in shades of orange.

'The colour of sunrise,' says Dad.

But I know why he really chose orange; it was Mum's favourite colour.

After several coats, the grey stains of dead spiders, flies and dust are completely gone. Once the painting is done and the windows cleaned, everything looks a bit brighter.

Each day, Dad walks to town and brings the donkeys up laden with a piece of furniture, fabrics or food supplies.

'Managed to hire any staff to help?' Grandma asks on the sixth day, as she's hanging a recycled sari on the wall to cover a large crack.

Dad shakes his head.

Even without any help, the hotel is looking much better than before. I stand on a chair to hang curtains in the living room. Once we unroll patterned rugs over the bare concrete floors, the hotel feels warmer. Dad evens fills the bookcase with books from town about the local area.

'Not too bad,' says Dad, stepping back to admire the work. 'Not too bad at all.'

He places his arm over my shoulders.

'All we need now is to make the guestroom beds,' says Grandma. 'Mr Bhat and Mr Anand will be staying for a few weeks to help oversee the opening, right?'

Dad nods and we use new bedspreads with swirling paisley patterns, and cushions with silk covers in their rooms. I make sure there are candles and oil lamps in every room, although Dad assures me there will be electricity soon.

For the finishing touch, Dad displays Caspar the taxidermy python above the front door, as if he's guarding the hotel. Once he's finished hanging Caspar, we both collapse down on the sofa and I rest my head on his shoulder.

'I think they'll be impressed,' says Dad.

The next day, Mr Bhat and Mr Anand arrive later than expected, puffing and sweaty from the walk up the hill. Polly barks and growls at them.

Mr Bhat has a thick neck and a voice as slippery as butter. I nickname him Toad after the cane toads in Australia. Mr Anand is tall and skinny and has a whispering edge to his voice. With his eyes darting around the trees outside, he reminds me of a wasp. I call him Stinger.

Stinger stops outside the gate, running his hand up and down a tree trunk.

'You've had a visitor,' he says, beckoning to me. 'You see these scratches?'

I nod.

'They're leopard markings.'

I shiver. I wonder if a leopard followed us home from Praveen's last week.

'Let's start the tour,' says Dad, clapping his hands together. 'Now that the water's been connected, everything's ready for guests except the electricity.' Grandma and I follow behind them.

As we walk upstairs, Toad jumps suddenly. I follow his line of sight. Georgina the Spider is on the wall next to him. Toad pulls a rolled-up newspaper from his pocket and raises his arm.

'No,' I shout, jumping in front of him. 'Don't!'

'Why on earth not? Our guests won't want pests in their rooms biting them in the middle of the night,' he says, sidestepping around me, the newspaper still raised.

'But that's Georgie,' I say. 'House spiders don't bite humans and they can live for eight years. Don't kill her,' I say desperately. I frown at Stinger. 'I thought you liked wildlife.'

'I told her about the sanctuary where you worked,' explains Dad, smiling.

'Mammals were my speciality,' he replies through his teeth. 'Tigers and elephants. Not spiders.'

'Let's move on,' says Dad quickly. He ushers the bosses towards the hallway.

On we walk through the newly painted and furnished hotel. They don't seem to notice all our hard work, or say how nice it's looking. They don't seem interested at all.

With each room we enter, Dad's posture slumps a little more.

'Would you like to see your bedrooms?' I ask. 'I think you'll like them.'

'We're not staying here,' Toad replies, shortly. 'We're staying in the cabin.' I remember the building Praveen pointed out when we were in the woods last week.

'Let's leave them to it and go to the festival,' Grandma whispers to me and I nod, grateful to be leaving the bosses and their snide attitude behind. On our way out I make sure the door to my bedroom is locked. Joey is sleeping, and I don't want Toad and Stinger to disturb her. There's something about them that makes me uneasy.

CHAPTER FIFTEEN

Holi

The town is transformed by the festival of Holi. It brims with people. The noise of drums, whistles and chatter fills the air. Shops sell big pots on the roadside containing brightly coloured powders.

'Are they spices?' I ask Grandma.

'No,' she says, laughing. 'They're Holi colours.' She scoops blue, pink, red, green and orange powder into bags and hands them to me.

I'm about to ask her what they're for, when something sprinkles over the side of my face. I jump and spin around, bringing my hand to my cheek. My fingers come away purple. Praveen's laughing nearby, also holding bags of colours. Flecks of pink land in Grandma's grey hair.

'I get it,' I say. 'Thanks, Grandma!'

I take the colours and dart off to get Praveen back. I flick him with orange.

All around us people are already covered in multi-coloured paint splodges. Colours fly through the air.

I'm a few feet behind Praveen, when he turns and throws a whole bag at me. I duck and it hits a middle-aged man in a suit getting out of a taxi instead.

'Hey!' shouts the man.

Praveen runs off again and I follow him, dashing down an alleyway. Someone tips a bucket of powdered paint over both of us from a balcony above. Covered in colour, we stop and lean against the wall laughing.

A car speeds past the opening to the street in a flash of noise and a rush of air.

A car, going too fast.

Suddenly my stomach hurts.

I bend over, squeezing my eyes shut and resting my hands on my thighs.

Mum and I are singing at the top of our lungs along to the radio with the windows rolled down. The air is finally cooler outside. The evening sun is bright behind us. Mum's driving me to my first official piano lesson. I've been teaching myself for years.

Mum taps the window frame in time with the music. The wind blows her short hair back and fluffs it up.

'You look like a topknot pigeon,' I say.

'Why, thank you,' she replies. 'They're one of my favourites.'

I laugh.

'I think we might have just missed our turning,' says Mum. She bends forward to get her phone out of her bag.

'Again?' I ask, teasing her.

'Just get the map up, will you?' she says with a grin, passing me the phone.

We approach a roundabout. It's clear. I look down at the phone.

'Yeah, we were supposed to turn back there,' I say, looking behind us.

'No problem. I'll just go all the way around.' She pulls out and drives around the roundabout.

We exit and join the road again.

'We're going the right way now,' I say, *checking the map again.*

I glance up and see a truck fly round the corner towards us, straddling the centre of the road.

'Mum,' I say.

It keeps going.

We keep going.

And then there's nothing but blackness.

'You all right?' asks Praveen, and I snap back to myself, leaning against a wall and covered in colour.

'Yes, fine,' I reply. I wait a second for the tingling in my fingers to subside before I straighten up. 'Let's go.'

Everyone said it was a freak accident. It was the other driver's fault. The low sun was shining in his eyes as he turned the corner. He didn't see our car.

But all I think is what if I had never begged for those piano lessons. Mum would still be here now.

I catch my reflection in a shop window. My whole body is coated in splashes of red, orange, blue, green and pink, but my face looks drained of colour.

The doctor said it's normal to replay the accident, even to relive it, and that I shouldn't be scared when it happens.

But how can I not be?

Back on the street, the tarmac roads are splattered with colour, as are the cows wandering up and down. My heart still feels like it's beating too fast but when a red monkey with a bright blue tail swings past on a balcony, I smile and the feeling of tightness in my chest eases a little. Praveen buys us bottles of lychee juice from a street stall and we climb up to a rooftop and sip the juice through straws, watching the street below.

'You've been quiet since we left the alleyway,' says Praveen. 'Want to talk about it?'

I shake my head. 'I guess it feels strange to be playing games when there's so much going on and so much to do at the hotel.'

'We can go back if that's what you want?'

'No.' I move close to the edge and watch the people throwing paint on each other below. 'I dare you to empty the rest of your paint on one person.'

'You're on,' he replies. 'Only if you do it too.'

I wait until a relatively clean man walks underneath and tip the bag upside down.

'Good shot,' says Praveen.

The man looks up and we duck and laugh.

'We can only do this once a year,' says Praveen, grinning. 'May as well make the most of it.'

He takes my palm and draws a zigzag across it in green. My skin prickles under his touch.

CHAPTER SIXTEEN

Intruder

That night I wake up to a banging sound, as if someone is throwing something against the front door.

The moneylenders. They've tracked us down.

And then I remember that we're on a haunted mountain.

'Dad?' I squeak, switching on the torch by my bed. 'Grandma, can you hear that?'

Steeling myself, I pull the duvet back and slide out of bed. As I head out of my room, the noise gets louder.

Then I hear a scratching, like forks scraping across china plates. It sends shivers down my spine.

'Grandma?' I hiss, tiptoing into her room.

'What?' She sits up and hears the noise. 'Don't move,' she says. 'Stay here. I'm getting your dad.'

'Here,' I say, handing her the torch. 'Take this.' Dad's room is downstairs.

As soon as she leaves it's dark.

I can't stay here alone, not in the dark. Feeling my way in the blackness I stumble after her, down the stairs and into the kitchen. I collide with Grandma in the doorway and we both gasp in fright.

I smell the boiled meat Grandma cooked for Polly earlier.

There's a thump against the front door and

I yelp. Polly barks at the door, gnarling and showing her teeth.

'Dad!' I scream.

Dad flies out of his bedroom.

There's another thump. The door shakes.

'Get back,' he says, ushering us behind him.

'Can . . . whatever it is get in?' I ask Grandma.

She shakes her head.

The scraping stops. It's replaced by a low growl.

'What is it?' I whisper.

Dad pauses. He switches on another torch and grabs a saucepan from the cupboard.

'Get back,' says Dad again, and he bangs against the inside of the front door with the saucepan.

I peer through the window. It's pitch black outside but from the glow of the kitchen I glimpse the giant outline of a creature on its hind legs.

'It's a bear!' I say.

Dad pounds against the wood again.

'Careful you don't break the door. It's the only thing between us and that animal,' says Grandma.

My heart thuds.

'It's after the dog meat,' says Dad. 'Get it out of here.'

Grandma lifts the pressure cooker full of meat and whisks it away.

Dad clashes two saucepans together. I do the

same and we bash them until all I can hear is the ringing of the metal.

Dad stops and holds out his hand. I keep the saucepans still. He juts his head forward, listening.

It's quiet.

'I think we scared it away,' says Dad.

I peek out the window. The bear is leaving. It strides on all fours away from the house, pausing once to look back at us.

If only I had my camera.

I know that's what Mum would be thinking too, right now.

Grandma ushers me away from the window.

'We mustn't leave any food out, okay?' says Dad.

We both nod.

'I'll reinforce the door in the morning. Can't have the guests being eaten by bears in their sleep now, can we?' says Dad, trying to joke. He smiles, but his voice cracks.

Grandma puts her arm around him.

'Maybe coming here was a mistake. I thought this job would be perfect,' Dad says, clasping the back of his neck. 'But there's so much to do.'

'Nonsense,' says Grandma, pulling the kitchen chairs out for us to sit down. 'We'll have guests in no time.'

Grandma lights a candle, brings milk to boil

on the stove and makes us cocoa. I watch the steaming chocolate swirl in the mug. It's too hot to drink.

'We just need some staff,' says Dad. 'If only I could convince some of the locals to work here.'

'You will,' says Grandma. 'They'll soon realise there's nothing to be afraid of here.'

I look at Dad and recognise suddenly how tired and worn he looks. Everything is riding on the hotel being a success and him keeping his job. I'm still angry at him but I don't want him to struggle. Besides, it's not so bad here; I think I might be starting to like it, a bit. I've even arranged to meet Praveen again in the morning.

'They'll come,' I say, resting my head against Dad's shoulder. 'I'm sure of it.'

But I'm not really. All I know is that if they don't come, Dad won't have a job.

And then where will we go?

CHAPTER SEVENTEEN

Mystery

'I brought you a picture of Durga,' says Praveen.

We're sitting in his tree; I slipped away after breakfast without anyone noticing. Dad was busy writing flyers to advertise for the position of a chef, while Grandma placed hanging flower baskets along the veranda as she waited for her rhododendron jam to cook.

Praveen's flock munch on the grass beneath us.

He passes me a colourful postcard of a warrior goddess with long dark hair, riding a tiger. She has eight arms, each hand carrying a weapon to destroy, or a tool to create. I stare at the picture. She doesn't look like a ghost at all. She looks strong and full of life.

'I like her,' I say.

'You can keep it,' he says. 'She reminds me of you in that picture.'

I smile.

'I've been thinking – about the curse on the mountain and how you could try and protect yourselves. One thing we could do is build a shrine to the Goddess Durga somewhere close by. To say thank you for allowing us to be up here, and to ask her to let your father run the hotel in peace. What do you think?'

'Can't hurt,' I say with a shrug.

Birds scatter from the tree into the sky and I jump.

Praveen raises a finger to his lips. 'Something's coming,' he whispers.

I sit still, listening to my heart pound in my ribcage. I hear the crunch of footsteps.

Dad.

I feel suddenly guilty that instead of helping Dad and Grandma in the hotel I'm sitting in the tree with a boy.

'Better go. Bye,' I whisper and wave at Praveen, preparing to climb down the trunk.

I pause with my foot in mid-air.

There's more than one set of footsteps.

I grip the tree to steady myself and peer down through the leaves.

Mr Bhat and Mr Anand are walking towards the cabin.

Something about the way they look around as they reach it gets my attention. Stinger checks over each of his shoulders, as if he's afraid of someone seeing him.

I glance at Praveen and see he's watching them too, his dark eyes thoughtful.

'What don't you want anyone to see?' I ask them under my breath.

Stinger unlocks the padlock. They step inside and the door swings shut behind them.

I stare after them. It's a very large padlock for a cabin.

I shimmy down the tree trunk.

'Where are you going?' hisses Praveen.

'I want to see something,' I reply, softly thudding to the ground. 'Keep a look out.'

I approach the cabin and, keeping my head mostly under the sill, try to peer through the dusty window next to the door. It's too filthy to see into.

There are thuds and muffled voices before footsteps head towards me. I step backwards as the door flings outwards. For a second, the door shields me from sight and I dive behind the side of the cabin. As the door opens a strange smell wafts into the air, a smell like rotting leaves.

They stride outside.

I'm hidden from sight among the bushes, but I can just see Stinger. He's staring out over the hills and humming to himself. I hear Toad close the padlock over the latch and as he begins to walk away, I peek around the side of the cabin and watch them leave. I see what they're carrying.

'Guns,' I whisper.

CHAPTER EIGHTEEN

Secrets

As soon as their backs are turned, I glance up at the tree.

Praveen pokes his head out through the leaves.

'I'm going to follow them,' I mouth, gesturing at the bosses, then I sneak after them, ducking behind trees and crouching next to bushes.

They're striding straight towards the hotel.

There's something the bosses are hiding and one way or another, I have to find out what it is.

Toad and Stinger reach the hotel and disappear inside.

I hesitate for a minute then peer in through the kitchen window, just in time to see Toad pass the guns to Dad.

Why does Dad want guns?

I duck back down again, my heart racing. Grandma and Dad used to go clay pigeon shooting in Australia but apart from that I've never seen my dad with a gun.

I hear the door slam and watch Toad and Stinger walk down the path.

I think for a moment about what to do then step into the kitchen.

'Why do you need guns?' I ask.

For a second I think Dad looks guilty but the expression is gone in a flash. 'It's just a precaution,' he says. 'Mr Bhat has a special licence to keep them in case any animals attack the guests.'

'Is this because of the bear?' I ask.

'That's right. We should be prepared in case it comes back.'

I remember my feeling of helplessness when the bear was at the door. It does make sense to have some sort of protection around, just in case.

'Anyway,' he continues, grinning, 'I've got news for you.'

'What is it?' I ask.

'By tomorrow night, we'll have electricity.'

'Really?' I ask, stroking Joey, who has hopped into the room. The walls are covered in a web of wires all leading out the window into a knot dangling from a tree.

Dad nods. 'And look what I found in town.' He leads me to the living room where Grandma is seated on the couch sewing, and points to a box covered by a patterned bedspread. 'Ta-da!' he says, lifting the material to reveal a boxy television set. 'We'll never get a signal up here but we can watch films. I had the idea as soon as I saw it.'

'I didn't bring any films,' I say.

Dad grins and hands me a DVD.

I stare at the box. It's got a picture of an Indian woman and man on the front, dancing.

'It's a musical?' I ask.

'It's Bollywood,' replies Dad and he starts

singing to himself. 'I picked it up in town. We could watch it tomorrow night.'

'Can I invite Praveen too?' I ask.

'If his parents don't mind.'

'Why don't you invite him for dinner beforehand as well?' says Grandma. She's been sewing several pillowcases together so that we can hang them around our necks and shoulders: a front pack, for Joey. 'Try this,' she says, passing it to me.

I fasten the straps and Joey jumps straight into it when I call her. She's much heavier now.

'It's perfect,' I say, sliding it off. 'I'll take her for a walk in it later.'

I turn and grab a banana on the way out. Then I stop. 'Hey Dad,' I say. 'Promise me there'll be no more secrets. Even if something bad happens. You can tell me. We're in this together now.'

'No more secrets,' he says, wiping his hands on his trousers. 'Trust me.' He smiles and waves, but as I pause in the doorway and look back, I see that his face is now drawn and worried.

And I realise that's the problem. I *don't* trust him. No matter how hard I try, after everything that happened in Australia with the moneylenders, there's still a part of me that doesn't.

A big part.

I make my way back to the tree. Praveen is probably long gone by now but I want to check.

'Praveen?' I call.

There's no reply and no sign of the flock.

I climb up into the branches and hear a squeaking sound.

'Bandar?' I ask, softly.

The baby monkey peers down at me. Her face is starting to get the white tufty mane around it that I've seen on the older monkeys. I offer the banana and she swings down and snatches it out of my hand before climbing back up.

'Don't worry,' I whisper to her. 'Your mum will come back for you soon.'

I sit in the tree for a while, in case Praveen shows. I feel like I'm trespassing, being here without him.

I gaze around. The mountain is covered in pieces of shiny grey slate. The same slate the roofs in the village are made of. I climb down and with a chalky stone I write a message to Praveen on some slate, before propping it against a branch in the tree. He'll discover it when he feeds Bandar in the morning.

On the path back to the hotel, I see three figures ahead. I recognise Toad and Stinger's outlines straight away but there's a third person with them too. As I get closer I realise I've never seen the man with them before; he's dressed in walking boots, a thick woollen sweater, a raincoat and a hat. He's carrying a big backpack with a saucepan hanging from it.

Toad passes him a small box. It catches the sunlight in his hand and gleams.

I squint and quicken my pace, straining to see what it is. It's a tin. It looks familiar. I remember tracing the pattern with my fingertips the night I first arrived.

The tin with claws in it.

The men fall silent as they notice me.

'Good morning,' I say, trying to sneak a better glance at the tin as I pass, but the man quickly tucks it into his pocket.

Stinger smiles and replies, 'Good morning,' but Toad just grunts.

As soon as I'm out of sight, I hurry back to the house. The kitchen is empty but I can hear Dad and Grandma moving about upstairs. I remember the exact drawer where I found the tin the night we arrived; I slide it open and rummage through the cooking utensils. I search every corner. My heart pounds.

The tin's not there.

CHAPTER NINETEEN

Lights

The next evening Grandma cooks *aloo channa*, a potato chickpea curry. The spices fill the air, and make my stomach rumble. Grandma used to make these dishes in Australia but everything tastes different here – a bit stronger.

There's a knock on the door and I open it to Praveen. 'You got my message,' I say, beaming. 'There's something I want to tell you.' I lower my voice and usher him in, explaining about the man in trekking clothes and the tin with claws in it.

'I wonder what kind of claws they were,' says Praveen. 'Some animal claws are illegal and worth a lot of money.'

'Why would the bosses leave them in the kitchen then?'

Praveen shrugs. 'They used the house more before you arrived. Maybe they left them there accidentally.'

'Is that Praveen?' calls Grandma from the kitchen. 'Perfect timing! Dinner's ready.'

'Not a word to Dad,' I say quickly as we walk through to the dining room. 'I haven't told him.'

He nods.

After we sit, Grandma hands us bowls of steaming rice and curry.

'The hotel looks great,' says Praveen.

'I'm glad someone thinks so,' replies Dad

and I know he's thinking about Mr Bhat and Mr Anand.

As the sun sets, Dad looks at his watch. 'We should have electricity by now. Shall we give it a try?' He smiles at me. 'I want you to do the honours, Ruby.' He opens his arms in a big gesture. 'The grand light switching on.'

I laugh. It reminds me of Christmas.

'Let's count down,' says Grandma. 'Three. Two. One. Go!'

I flick the switch.

The lightbulbs flash on. Barely. It's the dimmest glow I've ever seen.

'We might have to get some lamps too,' says Grandma, after a pause.

In the distance I hear a monotonic toot toot sound.

'Do you know what makes that noise?' I ask Praveen, glancing out of the window. 'I hear it every night.'

'A collared owlet,' he replies. 'It's a type of pygmy owl.'

I'm still looking out of the window when I see the green light bobbing outside, closer by this time, about twenty feet away. It creates a moving green glow around the trees. I look for the shape of a person, but only see the twisted long shadows of branches, stretched and distorted. I yank the curtains shut. Even if it is just a shepherd, there's still someone – or something – out there, in the darkness.

Dad is on his hands and knees turning the TV on.

'I picked out a present for you in town,' says Grandma, as Dad fiddles with the TV. She hands me a piece of blue silk material. 'It's a scarf.'

'Thanks,' I say, rubbing the silky fabric between my fingers and tying it around my neck.

'No, not like that. Come here.' She drapes it over my shoulders.

'There,' she says, standing back to admire her work. 'Beautiful.'

I move to the one mirror in the house, and stand on tiptoe in an attempt to see down to my feet. I haven't examined my reflection in ages. My hair's grown and I look older. I gather my hair with my fingers and tie it in a ponytail, the same way Mum did before she cut hers. I turn my face to the side, seeing parts of her staring back at me.

We all jump as the TV suddenly blares with Indian music and singing.

'It works!' says Dad, straightening up.

'That's Garjan Mankar,' says Praveen, pointing at the screen. 'He's famous. He always dances like this.' Praveen copies his dance moves.

'I know that one,' says Dad. And to my horror

he joins in, flinging his arms up and down into the air.

Grandma sways from side to side, swishing her hips back and forth, singing along with the song and beckoning me to dance too.

I flop down on the sofa, cringing with embarrassment.

Dad grabs my hand and dances with it.

'All right,' I say eventually. 'I'll stand.' I secretly want to have a go; they look like they're having fun.

I attempt to follow Praveen's arm movements, get it wrong and laugh.

'Come on!' he says, his dark eyes sparkling. 'Try again.'

I lift my hands and copy him, watching the way his hair falls over his forehead as he moves. We meet eyes.

'That's it! You've got it,' he says. His hand grazes my arm as we pass each other.

Grandma twirls around me.

The song finishes and everyone claps and cheers. I dart back to the sofa, laughing and out of breath.

Between them, Grandma, Dad and Praveen translate the film and I get an idea of the love story playing out in front of me. Soon Dad drifts off on the sofa and starts snoring gently but I'm so caught up in the film I hardly notice.

After an hour, Grandma sniffs and I realise she's crying at the ending.

'My mum always cries at this part too,' says Praveen.

When the film's over, as Praveen is about to leave, he turns to me, lowering his voice so only I can hear. 'What do you think about building the shrine tomorrow?'

I hesitate, and then nod. Maybe it will help things for Dad and keep the green lights away from us.

He grins. 'I'll meet you by the tree in the morning. Bring some things as offerings.'

'Okay,' I say, grinning back.

As he turns to leave I say, 'Wait. I don't know how to build a shrine. What do I bring?'

'Don't worry about that,' he replies. 'Anything you bring will be perfect. You'll be able to tell.'

Later, as I'm helping Dad with the dishes, I think of Praveen and the shrine and I can't stop smiling.

CHAPTER TWENTY

Shrine

I drift off to sleep that night still smiling. But I'm shortly jolted awake. Raised voices sound from the corridor downstairs.

I throw the blanket off and slide out of bed. Tiptoeing down the stairs, I peer round the door and see Dad sitting on the porch, talking to someone outside. I can't hear what he's saying but I can tell he's angry. I creep closer, but as I do Dad pushes his chair back and storms inside. I flatten myself against the wall as he strides away, into his bedroom.

I sneak to the porch, and see Toad and Stinger outside, silhouetted by a candle, murmuring together. Their fur coats are slung over the back of their chairs. I sidestep into the shadows. The night air is fresh and still.

'Do you think he'll blow it?' Stinger is saying.

'No,' says Toad quietly. 'He'll lose everything if he does.'

They clink glasses together before gulping their drinks and pouring more.

The owl toots in the distance.

There's a movement by my foot. Joey has followed me. Before I can grab her, she hops outside and bounces straight up to the men, knocking over one of their glasses with her tail. The glass smashes to the ground, sending the liquid all over Toad's fur coat.

'Stupid creature!' snaps Toad. 'That thing belongs on a wall.'

I rush forward and scoop Joey up in my arms, glaring at them.

'It was an accident. Joey didn't mean it.' I mutter.

'Do you know how expensive this is?' shouts Toad, pointing at the coat.

'Shouldn't you be in bed?' asks Stinger, smirking at me.

'No,' I say, lifting my chin. There's no way I'm letting the bosses tell me what to do.

They watch me leave. Stinger stands and closes the door behind me. I press my ear against it but their voices are muffled.

'How do you know Mr Bhat?' I ask Dad the next morning. He's outside, bending over the potatoes he planted. The soil has been dug up around them.

'I've known him for years — since before I knew your mum. When I was starting out in the hotel business, he was already established. He helped me get my first job. We're old friends.'

'You don't seem like old friends,' I reply.

'Especially when you were arguing last night.'

'You heard us?'

I nod.

He sighs. 'I'm sorry, Ruby. They told me I could run this hotel as if it was my own but now they want me to have a guest who I'm uncertain about, that's all.'

I shrug. Maybe that's all there is to it, but I'm not sure. Dad sounded so angry last night.

All in all, I'm glad that Praveen and I are building a shrine to Durga today.

Dad picks something off the dirt and straightens. It's a quill. 'The porcupine has been at my potatoes again. Half of them are gone.'

'Can I take that?' I ask, thinking about the offerings.

He passes it to me. I look around for other things to bring. Orange lilies that Mum would have loved grow by the front gate and I pick them, then place the stems in a glass of water.

Soon I have my notebook, in case a letter or picture is needed, a small tub of Grandma's jam and some rupee coins Dad left on the mantelpiece.

I carry it all to Praveen's tree. He's there already, sitting with his back up against the trunk. The flock surrounds the tree, bleating and munching through the grass around him.

'Ready?' he asks, standing up and eyeing my

gifts. I think he approves because he gives a little smile, especially when he sees the jam.

I nod. 'What did you bring?'

'Mainly food,' he says showing me a plate, wrapped in gold tinsel, and full of uncooked grains. I wonder if I should have decorated my offerings too.

'But I also found this,' he says and opens his palm. A butterfly wing rests on his skin.

I stroke it. Butterfly dust sticks to my fingertips. I blow it over my offerings.

Praveen whistles and the flock follows behind us as we move off the path, stepping through the thick foliage. We search for a hidden place in the forest to make our shrine. The air sings with birds and a jungle crow flies alongside us, cawing.

As we explore, I see a big bird's nest balanced in a tall deodar tree. I catch Praveen's arm. 'Look up there,' I say.

'It might be a vulture nest,' he says, his eyes shining.

I feel a quiver of excitement that I spotted something here on the mountain that Praveen isn't already familiar with. I'm beginning to learn about the mountain for myself. I think back to the first day, when I got lost, and how much more I now know.

I know that one side of the mountain is

covered in evergreen forest and the other is thick jungle with moss and vines. I know the plants that Grandma showed me, like the musk rose with its tiny white petals and heady scent, and the tall, straight deodar trees. I know about the paradise flycatcher bird that flies through the forest with a long, white tail gliding behind it.

'How about here?' I ask, stopping at a large flat boulder. Lizards scamper under it.

'Perfect.'

Praveen pulls out another postcard with a picture of the Goddess Durga on it and sets it at the top of the boulder.

'I have a copy too,' he says and smiles.

We lay out all the offerings, our multi-coloured assortment of presents, beneath, and I can't stop thinking of Mum and the way we celebrated her birthday this year by buying the flowers she loved and eating her favourite foods.

Praveen and I sit either side of the gifts on the warm boulder, while the goats rustle through the undergrowth around us. A ladybird lands on the postcard.

Then Praveen kneels directly in front of the postcard, presses his palms together and prays under his breath. It reminds me of how I used to talk to Mum aloud after she died. I stopped when I couldn't bring myself to picture her any more.

Praveen finishes and we sit in silence while the crickets chirp around us.

'Do you think it worked?' I ask.

He laughs. 'We'll have to wait and see.'

He looks at the sun setting in the sky and frowns. 'I have to move the flock,' he says. 'Can I walk you back to the tree?'

I shake my head. 'I think I might stay here for a bit.'

He waves and dashes down the slope, disappearing into the shadows of the jungle, calling the goats behind him. I sit still and listen to the wind rustling through the trees and the birds singing above me. After a while I take out my notebook and write to Mum.

Mum. I know I haven't spoken to you in a while. I picked these flowers and brought this jam for you.

Dad says you'll always be able to find me wherever I am. But just in case, hopefully this shrine will guide you to me. You were always very bad at directions.

Apparently the Goddess Durga protects the mountain. Maybe you can be friends. Love, Ruby.

When I get back to the house, the trees are full of grey langurs with black faces and white manes framing them. They strip the leaves off the branches and stuff them into their mouths. Polly stands on her back legs, front ones resting against a tree, tail wagging back and forth. Dad's building a fence around the potatoes. I spot another quill and twist it into my hair again.

'Where's Joey?' I ask Grandma, who's attempting to chase the monkeys out of the garden.

'She's in your room. She likes to spread out on the floor now she's getting bigger.'

I head inside to check on her. She's sleeping beside my bed and I kneel to stroke her soft nose. She wakes and leaps into my arms before following me outside.

I remove the camera from around my neck and snap a picture of Dad and Grandma in front of the monkeys. Grandma takes one of me, Dad, Polly and Joey. Dad draws me close and I smell spice on his breath. A butterfly, with markings similar to the wing that Praveen found, flutters in front of us and a hint of happiness bursts inside my chest. We're here, together, and that's all I really need to worry about.

CHAPTER TWENTY-ONE

School

'We're nearly out of drinking water again,' says Dad the next day, strapping a large container to his back. 'I'm going to the spring - want to come?'

I nod. I've always wanted to see the spring, set high up in the mountains.

'Be back before dusk — remember the leopards live in that area,' says Grandma. 'Take a torch. And Polly.'

'Walk in front of me, in case you slip,' says Dad once we're outside, hiking on the narrow path.

Polly creeps beside us, low to the ground, stopping and sniffing the air along the way.

I scan the trees for signs of leopard markings.

The path ascends and we climb upwards before it levels out and I hear the trickle of water. The natural spring turns out to be a pipe jutting out of the side of the slope, with water pouring into a concrete pool below.

'Where does it come from?' I ask.

'Deep in the ground,' says Dad. 'It's safe to drink because there's nothing to contaminate it. Although animals use it too, so we still need to boil it first.'

He kneels down. 'Pass me your container.'

I hand it to him and Dad holds it under the running water until the container overflows and he switches it with his.

'Hey Ruby,' he says.

'What?'

'I've been thinking. There isn't going to be much for you to do up here.'

I laugh. 'There's loads. Look.' I tell him what Praveen told me about the insects and the birds. 'And look at this,' I say, unravelling the quill from my hair and handing it to Dad. 'Another porcupine quill.'

Dad looks at me, puzzled. 'Well, the thing is, I found this great school.'

I can do school. Maybe it's in Praveen's village.

'It's in the next state and you'll have to board — but it has a fantastic reputation.'

My heart sinks as I realise what he's saying. 'You don't want me here any more?' I ask.

'Oh sweetie, it's not that. Public schools don't start until September. It's only June. What are you going to do until then? You need to do something with your time.'

I clench my fists into a ball. 'I *am* doing something . . .' I grab my camera and flick through the photos. 'Look.' My voice echoes around the mountains.

'Your mother went to boarding school,' he says, ignoring my photos.

'She hated it,' I say.

'That's not true. It will be good for you. You'll make lots of friends.'

I screw the lid on to my water bottle with shaking hands. 'You may as well have left me in Australia. I'm not going. Come on, Polly.'

I turn and run off through the trees.

'Ruby, wait!'

I hear Dad trailing behind with the heavy water container. I speed up; I don't want him to see my stinging eyes.

I run blindly until I realise I've reached the tree. It's the only place I feel like being right now. I don't want to talk to anyone; I'm even hoping Praveen's not there. I sit on one of the low branches with my head in my hands. Bandar climbs down and wraps her silky arms around me. She picks through my hair.

'I'm sorry I didn't bring any food,' I say, miserably. Seeing Bandar without her mum makes my chest ache with sadness.

'I hope she finds you soon,' I whisper.

A while later, the tree shakes as Praveen climbs up. 'What happened?' he asks as he sees my teary face.

'Dad's sending me away. I don't want to leave.'

'Where?' he asks, feeding Bandar fresh fruit and peanuts.

'Boarding school.' I straighten up. 'Maybe I could run away and become a shepherd like you.' I force a smile.

'Sure,' he says, but I know he's just trying to make me feel better.

'Can I learn a new word today?' I ask, trying to distract myself and thinking of Mum. 'What's snake?'

'*Saanp*,' he says.

'It has the same kind of sound,' I reply. 'I think I can remember it.'

'Is Australia very different to here?'

'Yes,' I reply. 'Where I lived it was dry and dusty and flat. So flat that you could watch the actual sun set on the horizon and the moon was huge when it rose.'

I reach for my necklace.

He catches it with his finger. 'That's pretty,' he says. 'Did you make it yourself?'

'Yes – it's a pebble. I found it with my mum,' I say.

'I found my staff with my dad. We carved it together.' He hesitates. 'Is she dead, your mum?'

I nod. 'Eighteen months ago.'

I remember the day Mum and I discovered the stone. We were walking through the outback together. Mum stopped to look at a desert rose and I saw something shiny on the rock in the ground. 'It might be an opal,' she'd said. We picked it up, took it home and cleaned it. It wasn't an opal, it turned out, just an ordinary stone with a hole straight through it. I was disappointed it wasn't special but then Mum threaded the string through the middle and fastened it around my neck. 'It is special,' she'd said. 'It's the perfect stone for a necklace.'

I've never taken it off.

A high-pitched calling starts up in the branches above me.

'Listen,' says Praveen, pointing into the air. 'The monkeys.'

They move in the trees around us. The leaves rustle and the branches spring back as the langurs jump from them.

'We should move,' says Praveen, climbing out of the branches and beckoning me down. We lean on either side of the trunk, looking up. The monkeys edge closer, calling to one another. A big one leaps into our tree. Bandar jumps into her arms, squealing, and they clasp hold of each other.

Praveen smiles at me.

Bandar grabs the long hair on her mother's belly. She looks down at us and meets our eyes as the mum bounds into the next tree, reunited with their troop.

'Bye, Bandar,' I whisper.

CHAPTER TWENTY-TWO

Guest

Dad's waiting for me when I get back to the house, along with Joey who bounces around me.

'I'm sorry, Ruby,' he says. 'I didn't mean to spring the idea of school on you. Please promise me you'll think about it. That's all I'm asking.'

I nod and his eyes lift.

He claps his hands together. 'Guess what? I hired our first staff member. A cook called Manjeet. With a cook, we can officially open!'

'We should celebrate,' says Grandma. She fetches jam and crackers from the kitchen.

I flop down on to the sofa with the wildlife book Dad gave me and read about leopards. Joey lies on the sofa next to me, resting her head on my knee. She squeaks and wrinkles her nose as she dreams. Polly sleeps on the other side of her.

Dad sits back into his chair in front of the fire, his face relaxed. I haven't seen him like this for an age.

The phone rings and Dad goes into the office to answer it.

He returns and sits staring into space, his jaw set.

'Who was that?' I ask.

'Mr Bhat has asked Garjan Mankar to stay here in order to drum up some publicity for the hotel. They know each other.'

I stare at him blankly. 'Garjan Mankar?'

He rummages around the television, finds the

Bollywood DVD we watched and hands it to me.

'The film star?' I ask. 'Really?'

Dad nods. 'Apparently he wants a mountain retreat away from the hustle and bustle of the city and the press.'

'Why aren't you more excited?' I ask Dad. 'This is great, isn't it?'

'I am, love,' says Dad. 'I'm just tired, that's all.'

The next morning, I wake up and wander to the kitchen to eat breakfast. Dad's already there; opening cupboards, scanning the food and writing a shopping list. He bends over the paper on the table and scribbles with a pen. The ink doesn't come out.

'Grab me another pen from the office, dear,' he says. 'But make sure you knock first, Mr Bhat and Mr Anand are in there organising Garjan's trip.'

'Sure,' I say. I'll take any excuse to spy on the bosses.

As I approach the office door, I notice it's ajar. Instead of knocking, I stand outside and listen.

'It's too risky,' says Stinger. 'Everything's

going so well – why would we jeopardise it with this stupid movie star?'

'He's going to pay a lot, more than—' Toad drops his voice and I can't hear the amount.

'Even so, are you sure it's a good idea?' replies Stinger.

'I found one,' shouts Dad from the kitchen, making me jump. 'And Praveen's here.'

The bosses fall silent and I back away quickly into the kitchen before they open the door.

I cook banana porridge and sit with Praveen on the veranda, filling him in on everything that has happened – about Garjan coming to stay in our hotel (he is a lot more impressed than I was) and about what I just overheard.

'They were talking about whether Garjun coming was a good idea,' I say between mouthfuls. 'But how could it be bad to have a movie star at the hotel? Maybe Dad thinks the hotel isn't ready for so much publicity . . .' I trail off.

Praveen nods thoughtfully. 'How well does your dad know the bosses?' he asks.

'He says they're old friends.'

Praveen looks at the floor.

'Why?' I ask. 'What is it? You can tell me.'

He meets my eyes. 'It's nothing concrete. It's just . . . I've had a bad feeling about them for a while.'

'Me too,' I say.

'And I've been thinking about the claws you said were in that tin, and how the only way to get them would be to kill an animal.'

'And they have guns,' I add. 'Dad says they're only for protection — but I'm not so sure.'

He nods. 'Exactly.'

'You think they might be . . . poaching?' I whisper under my breath.

'I don't know,' says Praveen. 'But I think we should find out.'

'How?' I ask.

'We can look for evidence,' says Praveen.

'I can take photos,' I say.

He nods. 'Let's document all their movements. And we need to get in that cabin somehow.'

'Let's start with a stake-out tomorrow,' I say. 'We'll hide in the tree and take photos of them coming and going.'

'It's a plan,' says Praveen.

But I see Toad sooner than that.

He bursts into the hotel later that day. Dad is in the hallway tinkering with the phone line.

'You can't hire someone without my permission!' he cries.

143

Dad puts down the screwdriver. 'What do you mean?' he asks.

'The reason I hired you was because I knew that back in Australia you ran a hotel by yourself, along with your wife. And that's what you have to do now. I don't want anyone else working here, is that clear?'

Dad's face flushes at the mention of Mum. He touches his wedding ring. 'We never discussed that,' he says steadily. 'Why don't you want any staff?'

Toad sounds calmer now too. 'We want to provide the guests with a fully immersive experience in nature amongst the animals here. No traditional hotel trappings.'

Dad laughs in disbelief. 'That doesn't make any sense. Do you know how much work it is, to run a hotel this size? And if you haven't noticed, Jean isn't with me, and my mother is eighty-four.'

'You'll figure something out,' says Toad.

'I have. I've hired Manjeet. He stays.'

'Go Dad,' I whisper under my breath. I see a glimpse of his old spark and the fieriness in him. I wonder if he's been secretly scared of things too since Mum died.

Toad scowls and his eyes bulge, but then he turns away. 'Fine,' he mutters. 'But no one else.'

I narrow my eyes at his retreating back.

Does he want to keep people away from here because they're poaching?

CHAPTER TWENTY-THREE
Smoke

I awake the next morning to Polly barking at me, and immediately taste wood smoke in the air. It clings to the back of my throat. Something is wrong.

I jump out of bed and race to the window. Grey smoke billows into the air, from further down the mountain.

'Dad!' I shout. 'There's a fire.'

Joey's fast asleep and snoring. I kiss her forehead before pulling on my jeans and darting downstairs, slipping my sweatshirt on over my T-shirt as I run. My shoes slap against the stairs.

The rooms downstairs are clean and empty. 'Dad!' I yell. Then I remember Dad and Grandma were going into town this morning to get supplies.

I can't wait for them. I need to find out where the fire is and if I can help.

As soon as I leave the hotel, I can tell the fire's coming from Praveen's village. I run down the path at full speed, Polly bounding beside me.

I cough as I get closer and hold my side; my chest is in stitches from running and I can't draw a clean breath because of the smoke. The air that was once full of butterflies is now full of sparks and embers.

I burst out of the forest and into the village. The trees and the stables closest to the forest are ablaze. The villagers have formed a line and are passing water-filled buckets to each other. Two men use hoses. They wet the ground around the fire to stop it from spreading.

I spot Praveen in the line and run towards him. 'Praveen!' I shout.

He sees me, and rushes over. His face and arms are filthy with soot.

'What happened?' I ask.

'They say one of those trees got hit by lightning and started a fire,' he says. 'The pine needles are flammable - it spread quickly.'

'Can I help?' I ask.

'Listen,' he says, looking over his shoulder as he leads me back to the path. 'You should get out of here. People are angry and upset. They think the fire was Durga's curse. They think she's angry.'

'Why?' I ask, my heart sinking.

'Because there are people on the mountain again.'

'They think this is our fault?'

'I — look, it's just better if you're not here right now,' he says, before turning and dashing back to help.

I stumble to the forest path and watch, hidden by the trees. Only when the flames are dampened and the trees are charred skeletons do I allow myself to turn home. And as I push my way through the jungle, I notice something on the mossy ground beneath me.

A purple match box.

That evening, I walk into the office as Dad slams down the phone.

'Manjeet says he can't take the job after all. The one person who'd agreed to work here just quit,' he says, rubbing the back of his neck. 'How am I supposed to run this hotel by myself?'

'I'll help,' I say. 'We'll run it, the three of us.'

Dad smiles at me faintly.

'Do you need me to do anything now?' I ask, desperate for something to take my mind off the idea that Praveen might think I'm to blame for the fire.

Dad shakes his head.

I stare out into the night. The lights are there again. Green flickers in the distance. I realise that Dad is standing next to me, watching them too.

'I'm starting to believe in this curse,' he says quietly.

'Mum would be laughing at you right now,' I say. Mum was always very scientific.

He smiles. 'I know.'

I watch his worried face.

What do I think about the curse?

I want to be like Mum, and think it's all rubbish. But the fire, the lack of staff . . . perhaps we really have brought bad luck to this place.

'What if someone started the fire in the village on purpose?' I ask Dad, voicing something that's been worrying me all day.

'But they didn't, darling. It was caused by lightning. There's nothing anyone could have done to prevent it.'

I reach my hand in my pocket and cup the purple matchbox.

CHAPTER TWENTY-FOUR
Blood

I wake the next morning at dawn, still on the sofa. Polly's lying across my feet and they've gone dead. Dad's covered me with the quilt. I rub my eyes and drag my feet off the sofa, flexing my toes to get the feeling back.

I hear voices and step to the window to see who it is. I don't know who would be awake this early.

It's Toad and Stinger. They stride through the garden, wearing backpacks and walking boots. Clearly they're going into the mountains. There's someone with them, about Praveen's height and build, but he turns away before I can see his face. Without thinking, I slip on my shoes, turn the door handle and push open the front door.

Outside, the air is crisp and birds sing. Walking quietly, I follow the bosses as they climb higher into the forest. They pause in a glade and I squint through the trees, trying to see who's with them. The person turns and I see him visibly.

It's Amul.

What's Praveen's cousin doing with the bosses?

I duck quickly behind a bush. Toad grabs Stinger's arm and they all go very still. Then, silently, they slip rifles from their backpacks, before carrying on.

I duck low to the ground and creep forwards, following the two men and the boy ahead. The

154

trees rustle and dappled light flickers around me. I step as silently as I can, avoiding twigs and crisp leaves. The group stops, and I dart behind a tree. I can't be seen. They have guns.

I flatten myself against the trunk and peer around it.

They're gathered by a thick tree, examining the base.

I know what they're looking for: some trace of the leopard. But leopards are elusive. Their spotted coats and padded feet allow them to hide in shadows. There are only five ways to find a leopard: you can track their paw prints; follow their scratches and scrapes; look for their scat; discover their scent markings; and listen for other animals' alarm calls.

'Over there,' says Amul, pointing ahead. He raises his finger to his lips.

They move on, quieter and quicker.

I wait until they're out of sight then dash to the trunk they were inspecting.

A line of ants runs down it. Next to them, etched into the bark, are claw marks. I touch the scratches. They're fresh. A leopard was here recently. I sniff. I don't detect a spray odour. It's a good sign that the claw marks are a few days old. I turn back in the direction of Toad and Stinger and hope with all my might that the leopard is far away by now.

I sneak after the group again and soon catch glimpses of them through the trees. The forest throbs with the buzz of cicadas and chirp of birds. As I step over a fern, I slip on a rock and scrape my palms breaking my fall. I freeze on the ground.

Did they hear me?

Between the fern leaves ahead I spot their legs. They've stopped in the path. My heart pounds. I imagine what I'll say if I'm caught. Or worse, I realise they could think I'm a leopard and shoot me.

Maybe I should shout now.

But I stay silent and through the parted fern, I watch. They're not turning to look at me; they're staring at something on the ground.

I sink lower and wait.

The men peer into the undergrowth around them, before heading off to the left, in a new direction.

I dart to the place where they'd stopped. There are paw prints in the dirt, pointing in the direction the men went. They're about eight centimetres long. The main pad has three lobes on the back of it. Four toe prints with no claws sit above the pad. They're lightly imprinted in the earth. It definitely belongs to a leopard; they tread gently. The back paw print shines. I bend and touch it. It's sticky and I pull my hand back.

My fingers come away deep red.

My breath catches.

Blood.

I wipe my shaky hands on my trousers. There's a leopard out there, injured. And I have to find it before they do.

Just then, there's a low, guttural growl — and it's coming from behind me.

The bosses spin around, pointing the guns in my direction. My heart hammers. I drop to my hands and knees. Twigs snap under my weight.

Did they see me?

There's nothing I can do but stay as still as possible.

They step towards me. Stinger stumbles over a rock and thuds against the earth loudly.

There's a flash of spots through the undergrowth.

'That's our chance gone,' says Toad, irritably. 'Now it knows we're here, we'll never find it.'

'We can split up and search more,' says Stinger.

It's quiet. I stay as still as I can. Something in the ferns catches my eye and I stare at it until my vision adjusts. Golden green leopard eyes pierce into my own. Fear ripples through me.

Its big jaw is slightly open, panting. Long white whiskers tremble. It's as still as a statue. I try to quieten my breathing. I can't be the thing that gives us away.

We both wait, opposite each other, crouching in the undergrowth, hiding from the men with the guns.

CHAPTER TWENTY-FIVE

Storm

At last I think enough time has passed for the men to have gone. The jungle is still around us.

The leopard rises and slinks away. There's a flash of red on its back paw. It turns back to look at me one last time before disappearing into the jungle.

On shaky legs, I stand and run as fast as I can down to Praveen's village. The sky has an eerie orange tint to it and thunder bubbles overhead. The pressure is building in the air. A storm is on its way.

Praveen will be feeding the goats at this time.

'Praveen!' I call, as I get to the stable. He's sweeping the inside.

'Hi!' he says, turning. 'What are you doing here?'

'I saw them,' I gasp. 'Toad and Stinger. I saw them tracking a leopard in the jungle.'

Praveen takes my arm and sits me down on a bench outside.

'Should I be here?' I ask, looking around the village. 'Do they still think I'm to blame for the fire?'

'Don't worry about that. Most people believe that it was simply lightning. Tell me about Toad and Stinger.'

I reach for the matchbox in my pocket. 'But it wasn't lighting. Someone did start the fire,' I say. 'I found this at the edge of the village.'

I pass it to him and he turns it over in his hands. 'Why would anyone want to start a fire?'

'I don't know,' I say. 'Praveen, the bosses had guns. They're definitely poachers.'

Praveen stares at me and I can see the excitement building in his eyes — excitement, and anger too.

'There's something else,' I say quickly. 'There was someone with them.' I pause. I'm not sure how to tell him.

'Who?'

'Amul.'

'My cousin, Amul?'

I nod, watching Praveen's face closely. His normally warm eyes look cold and distant.

'He wasn't holding a gun,' I add. 'But - but he was there with them and — and I think he might have been helping them . . .'

I trail off.

'Why are you saying this?' asks Praveen. And I realise his anger is directed at me, not Amul. 'It's lies. I *know* Amul wouldn't poach leopards.'

'I'm telling the truth,' I reply quietly.

'Are you trying to turn me against my cousin?'

'I'd never do that.' My thoughts spin.

Why doesn't he believe me?

'I have to finish feeding the goats,' he says, turning his back on me.

My insides rip.

'I thought we were in this together,' I say to his back. He doesn't respond.

I turn and walk back through the forest to the hotel, fighting back tears. The wind rustles through the trees and picks up the wisps of my hair.

I know Praveen cares about the leopards as much as I do.

How do I tell Dad and Grandma about Mr Bhat and Mr Anand?

What proof do I have?

None.

I realise I've nearly reached our shrine to Durga. As I get closer I see everything's blown away with the wind.

Our gifts are dotted amongst the leaves on the ground. I snatch them up then sit amongst the broken pieces and hug my knees to my chest.

A wave of helplessness hits me, just like it did after Mum died.

'I don't know how to do this any more. Why can't you still be here?' I whisper into the wind. 'You'd know what to do. You'd believe me.'

A scrap of paper from the note I wrote to Mum is fluttering on the ground.

I pick it up. It's torn and tattered and most of the words are smudged by the rain. The only legible words are *protects the mountain*.

I don't know why, but it sparks a little bit of belief in me again.

A loud clash of thunder makes me jump. In the distance, charcoal clouds gather into looming cauliflower shapes. I have to get back to the hotel before the storm hits. I turn back and run.

Halfway there, hailstones hammer down around me. They hit the ground and bounce, pinging in all directions. The sky darkens, even though it's still morning.

Lightning flashes as I reach the house. Dad is standing on the porch and I see his expression change to one of relief when he sees me. I dash inside and rip off my wet, cold jumper. Hailstones are caught on my neck and I brush them off.

The electricity cuts out then, and we're plunged into dimness. As the storm rages I stand under the covered veranda and watch the flashes fork through the sky. This storm is Durga's punishment. Her anger at the poachers, out there on her mountain. Anger at them rages through me too. I feel it from my hardened jaw to my icy fingertips.

CHAPTER TWENTY-SIX

Stalking

Early that evening, Toad pops into the kitchen. I've been sitting at the table, thinking about how I can prove what I know. I scowl at him from behind my mug of hot chocolate. Dad looks up from the chopping board where he's cutting up potatoes and greets him warily.

'Some people are coming to pick up a package tonight or early tomorrow morning from the cabin,' Toad says to Dad. 'We'll be there but point them in the right direction if they stop here first, will you?'

'Of course,' replies Dad.

I slip away from the kitchen. I want to see what this package is and who is collecting it. It could be proof.

I grab my backpack and fill it with binoculars, a torch, my raincoat and some snacks. Next I pack my tent and strap it to the backpack. Then I stash it all under the bed.

After dinner I tell Dad and Grandma I'm tired and hug them both good night.

'Remember, the film star's arriving the day after tomorrow,' says Grandma.

'I know,' I reply, before heading up the stairs.

Joey bounces towards me when I reach my room, trying to jump in the backpack.

'Not now,' I whisper, stroking her fur. I kiss her forehead. 'I'll be back soon.'

I stuff my bed with pillows to make it look like I'm sleeping and slip out of the front door, letting it gently click shut behind me.

I have to wait a second for my eyes to adjust to the night's blackness. I think of all the things the dark is hiding: the green lights, the bears, the ghosts. Now I've more things than ever to be afraid of. Even with my torch, the dark presses in on me and suddenly I feel faint.

For a while there is nothing. Then I wake up in darkness.

I turn to Mum and see that her eyes are closed. I shake her, gently, but she doesn't wake. I try to open the car door but it's jammed. Mum's phone's on the floor. With shaky hands, I reach down and pick it up. The screen is splintered into a million pieces. I press the power button.

'Please turn on,' I say to myself, fighting down rising panic.

A backlight glows and I let out my breath.

I ring an ambulance and talk to the operator and all the while I'm staring at Mum, sleeping next to me.

The metal of the car frame is dented and caved in around us. I don't think I'm hurt but I wouldn't know; my whole body feels numb.

The operator tells me not to move Mum. He asks me to stay on the phone but Dad's face flashes through my mind and I tell him I have to speak to Dad.

Then I ring Dad. My voice breaks as soon as I hear his. He stays on the phone as I hold Mum's hand and whisper, 'I'm here. It's all going to be fine.' I never take my eyes off the slight

rise and fall of her chest. Sirens wail in the distance. All that
matters is Mum and making sure she's all right.

Mum's face dissolves into the night around me.
I reach out a hand against the door to steady
myself and breathe deeply.

'Okay darkness,' I whisper. 'I'll make a deal
with you. Keep me safe tonight and I'll never be
afraid of you again.'

I take one step, and wait for something to
happen. It doesn't. I take another and another,
until I'm running towards the tree and the cabin.
I clutch my necklace to my chest.

Long shadows quiver and leaves rustle as I
pass.

I move silently and quickly through the forest,
not looking back.

Just get there, I say to myself, over and over again.

I reach the cabin and position myself to the
side of it, off the path and out of sight. Holding
the torch between my teeth, I set up the tent
and place it so it's hidden behind ferns. I gather
some more leaves and arrange them on top to
camouflage it.

I climb inside and lie on my stomach, checking
with the binoculars that I have a clear path to
the cabin. After getting my camera ready, all
that's left is to wait. I cup my chin in my hands,
propping myself up. The only sounds are my

breathing and the toot-toot bird. Adrenaline shoots through my body and I become aware of my own smell amongst the earth and the pine.

What would I smell like to a leopard?

The thought should terrify me, but as I rest my head against my arm and listen to the jungle moving around me, I find the sounds comforting and feel safe.

I wake to voices and jerk upright. I fell asleep. That wasn't part of the plan. The sky is showing the first signs of lightness. I must have been asleep for hours.

A woman and a man are approaching the cabin. She has a lime green scarf wrapped around her head. They're both dressed smartly, not in trekking clothes like the man who took the claw tin.

As they get near I take some pictures. The light isn't good but as the cabin door swings open I manage to get a hazy image. Then the bosses greet them and they go inside.

I wait for them to reappear for an age, watching through the camera. Eventually they emerge, carrying a bulky package, wrapped up in brown paper. Stinger comes running out after them with a big backpack and they carefully slide the package inside it. A corner of the brown paper rips and for a second I swear I see yellow material with spots on it.

I gasp. I have to see what's in that package. It could be my only chance to prove they're poaching. I remember meeting the leopard's green eyes with my own. I have to do everything I can to protect it.

I crawl out of the tent as quietly as I can and follow the man and woman all the way down the mountain. It's dawn now and orange clouds streak across the sky. The rain has brought out the slugs. They cover the path down from the mountain and are the biggest I've ever seen. I step over a squashed light brown one and have to stop and take deep breaths for a second.

In town they head towards the train station. It's busy but I keep sight of the lime green scarf and follow it.

They step on to the train at the platform. I hesitate for a second, then make my decision.

I duck down and weave my way through everyone to the train. Holding my breath, I jump through the door on to the carriage. I quickly walk to the end coach, feeling eyes on me. Every seat is taken. Some people are sitting on the floor.

A whistle blows and the train slowly chugs forward.

CHAPTER TWENTY-SEVEN

Train

I wind through the aisle looking for a flash of green. I scan the heads: a blue turban; orange hennaed hair; a long plait. My heart pounds. I have to find them before the next stop. Otherwise I might lose them for ever.

Finally, I spot them. The man clutches the backpack in his arms. He has wide shoulders and a waistcoat over a striped shirt. His hair is short and when he turns, I see his moustache. She wears a purple and green salwar kameez. I squeeze into the luggage rack at the end of the coach and watch them, taking a furtive photo while they stare out of the window. The blur of scenery whizzes by next to them.

As we travel further and further away from home the windows mist up with condensation until all I can see are raindrop patterns on the glass.

I miss the mountain as soon as I leave it. I thought the train would have stopped by now. I swallow and try not to think about how to get back. I reach into my pocket. I have a few rupee notes, not enough for a train ticket.

Someone has left a magazine behind and I flick through it, trying to calm my nerves. I pause at a picture of a man taken outside of a courtroom. He looks familiar. He's got slick black hair, pearly white teeth and he's wearing a smart black suit and tie. Reporters surround him and he's raising his hand in front of his face to shield himself from them.

It's the film star. The one who's coming to stay at the hotel. Garjan Mankar.

The article is written in Hindi. I tear the page out and stuff it in my pocket.

I can hear activity at the other end of the carriage and I peek over the top of the suitcase to see what's happening. A man in a smart uniform is making his way down the aisle, swaying to the rhythm of the train. The conductor. My heart starts beating fast. He stops at every row, grasping the overhead bar with one hand and examining people's tickets with the other.

He looks up and I duck, pushing myself as far back on to the luggage rack as I can. Fans whir overhead. It's hot, stuffy and packed full of people. I have a few minutes at most before he reaches me. But just as I begin to panic, the train starts to slow. I have no idea where we are; I only know that we've been on the train for hours. I slip out of the coach door to the space between the carriages. I squeeze past the food and drink sellers, putting them between me and the conductor.

'Chai, coffee, snacks,' one shouts.

'*Paani*, water, *paani*, water,' another says, following closely behind, her arms full of bottled water.

The window of the main door to the outside is flung wide open. I stick my head out and breathe in, hoping for the cool mountain air. But it's warm and humid.

Drops of rain sprinkle on to my face. Everywhere around me is flat. There are no mountains in sight. The train is pulling into a city with tall buildings and temples rising into the skyline. Panic shoots through my body.

I glance back at the green scarf lady. She stands and reaches for a bag above her. She and the man are getting off.

The door to the carriage clicks open and the conductor steps through, past the woman selling water. He stops next to me and nods, gesturing to see my ticket. I force a casual smile and open my backpack, pretending to search for it. My mind is racing.

What should I do?

I can't lose the man and the woman. They're my only chance to prove to Praveen that I was telling the truth and to protect the leopards. I think about what Mum would have done.

And just then, like magic, the train door opens directly in front of me. Before I can change my mind I step off the train, leaving the conductor standing in the doorway.

I walk quickly and don't look back, merging

with the crowd. Train stations are the busiest places I've ever been.

'Samosa. Pakora,' yells a food seller. I can smell fried food and smoke, and everywhere people are jostling and pushing past me.

I keep weaving through the crowds until I'm sure the conductor has lost sight of me, then I turn and watch people disembarking from the train, searching for the couple. Just when I start to think I might have lost them, they appear in the doorway. They step off and I run after them, charting the glimpses of green amongst the crowd. The pair leave the station and I follow, wandering through narrow stone passages with electric wires criss-crossing above our heads.

I stay back so they won't notice me, holding my bag above my head to keep dry from the rain, which is slowly lessening. Adrenaline shoots through my body as I travel further and further away from the train station. I try to keep track of the turns we're taking; I have to be able to find my way home. I hurry past a shop with bedspreads folded into squares, piled higher than me. Four people on one motorbike beep at me to get out of the way and I dart to the shadows. They splash through a puddle.

The narrow streets open out to a small square lined on two sides by shops. A blue sugarcane juice cart stands in the corner. Beyond it is the biggest river I've ever seen, as wide as four buses. Brown water gushes. It's the kind of current that could sweep you away in a second. The low early evening sun is reflected on the ripples. People are gathered on the steps by the banks in brightly coloured clothes. Women bathe in the river on one side, men on the other. In between them, in the middle of the river, wooden boats bob. People sit in them, chatting.

I scan the crowd frantically for the couple, spot them some distance away, and run after them.

They're going into a café on the waterfront. I bend over my knees to get my breath back. At least I know where they are, for now.

CHAPTER TWENTY-EIGHT
Ganga

I walk along the river, across the road from the café, waiting for them. I can't go in; I don't have enough money to buy anything. This close to the water's edge I can see people washing garments at the bottom of the steps. Above them, rows of colourful clothes hang down by the riverbanks to dry.

Finally the rain stops completely and people rush to the water, kneel by it and light candles on floating flowers. I step closer and a woman hands me one that's already lit.

'*Aarti*,' she says.

I look back at the café. The couple are still drinking tea inside. I cup the flower in my hand to stop the flame from going out and gently place it on the water like everyone else. I push it out in the current and it bobs on the surface.

The light of the candles reflects in the water. It's mesmerising. I wish Grandma was here to see it. Once I start wishing, I can't stop. I wish that Praveen believed me, that I had proof of the poachers and most of all that I could have Mum back, even for one second. Orange petals scatter across the water. I blow on the flower gently, enough to push it into the current. It joins the hundreds of others flickering on the water. I keep my eyes on it.

To my right there's a wall blocking off access to a section of the river bank, beyond which smoke is rising. And amidst the noise and chatter around me, I think I hear someone crying.

I creep closer, stepping over plastic and rubbish lining the water's edge. Birds flock around the boats, screeching and twittering. The water level is high. I can tell by the markings on the steps.

I reach the wall and peek over it. The bank on the other side is covered in smouldering ash and cow dung. Men are gathered around a boat piled high with kindling. They carefully place a wrapped up object covered in garlands of orange marigolds on top of the pile.

I edge closer, trying to figure out what it is. One of the men says a prayer and lights the kindling. The flame whooshes. Wood crackles.

That's when it clicks. It's a body. They're burning the dead.

Like they cremated Mum, at the funeral.

I turn and run. Images of the hospital fill my mind: its sterile white walls, the blue uniforms, the metal squeaky beds.

I dash towards the café and lean against the outside of it, catching my breath. Looking back at the river, I swear the level has risen even since I've arrived. I peer into café and my stomach drops. The couple have gone.

How could I have taken my eyes off them for even one second?

I turn, scanning the heads of everyone passing.

And, by some miracle, I spot a flash of green emerging from a shop.

The rain suddenly pounds down, as if a cloud has burst. It stings my cheeks and thunders against the road. The couple hurry, rushing along the road under a big umbrella.

The streets empty. Everyone shelters under overhanging roofs or in doorways but the couple continues hastening down the street.

I sprint after them, seeing the world through blurry eyes, as we head out of the city. I'm soaking already and my heart pounds. The sky is dark and stormy and purple tinged. The river swells and surges as I travel alongside it.

I can't stop thinking about the body on the pyre. Thoughts of Mum fill my head again. The last thing I remember before she was cremated were the roses on her coffin.

A factory stands by the side of the river. It has the word 'Tannery' written along the front. From over the road, I photograph the couple as they disappear inside the building. I cross the street, looking around me before trying to push the door open, but it's locked. I hesitate.

What now?

And then, suddenly, everything changes.

A blast of noise comes from behind me. I spin my head around just in time to see the river swell and burst. Water surges out of the banks.

I dart backwards, pressing myself against the wall of the factory. I shove the camera in my backpack, into the waterproof pocket. There's no time to do anything else. Screams fill the air. Water rushes towards me, filling every space. It's a strong current, a wave that knocks me down and dunks me underneath.

The water is icy. It fills my mouth and my nose, choking me and stinging the back of my throat. My ears pound. I fight my way to the surface and breathe, spluttering water.

I know what's in the river.

The bodies that lurk beneath.

And then I stop thinking and start swimming.

CHAPTER TWENTY-NINE

Snake

My arms splash and wave as I try to grab on to something. Objects brush against my legs. The current sweeps me into a woodland area and I reach for a tree and wrap both arms around it. I grip it tightly. I've got it.

I drag my body out of the water and shimmy up the trunk, spluttering and spitting, thanking Praveen for all the tree-climbing practice. I put each foot on a branch and plant myself firmly in the tree, the water swilling beneath my feet.

My body shakes. I look around me. There are other people in the trees too. In the water below, a man with a big grey beard is being swept towards the trunk of my tree, carried along by the water. I bend down and reach out to grab him but he misses my hand and is swept away, bashing into the next tree along. He scrabbles to hold on and this time he makes it.

There's movement in the branch by my right elbow. At first I think it's part of the tree moving in the wind but then I realise I recognise the long thin body, the way it coils and slithers and wraps itself around a branch. A viper.

I see more snakes, in the other branches. One with diamond patterns. A bright green, flatter one. The tree is full of them. They've all slithered up to escape the water like me. One hisses and I freeze.

After a second, it slips away, higher up into the branches above me.

My wet clothes drip into the rush of water below. I should be more scared than I am but I feel oddly calm. Maybe it's because I'm in shock, or maybe it's because the snakes remind me of Mum. I open the bag to check on my camera. It's safe and dry.

The land around me is swallowed by water. The tops of the buildings and temples poke out.

The older man in the next tree wrings his hair out. He's dressed in a bright orange cloth and I recognise him as a holy man, a sadhu. He shouts something in Hindi at me. I shake my head.

'I don't understand!' I say. And then: '*Saanp!*' I call. It's the only word I know that could possibly apply right now. The word for snake that Praveen taught me.

'You don't need to worry,' he shouts again, in English this time. His voice is gruff. 'Nature is having a truce.'

Despite what he says, I don't want the snakes to come too close. I let them know I'm here by gently tapping the branch with one finger, so that the vibrations carry through the tree. One slithers away slightly.

The rain stops.

I watch the raging water below and the objects

floating in it. Other people in the trees are also shouting across to each other. One man balances a calf across his lap.

'Now we wait for the waters to recede,' says the holy man. 'I've seen this happen before.'

I look out at the city. I can see the flat roof of the factory up the river, and beyond it the ornate towers of the train station. On the roofs and the tops of the buildings, people gather. A huge fire lights the sky. Embers fly into the air.

'They're trying to perform the cremations from the roof,' says the holy man.

'Now?' I ask. 'Really?'

'They've travelled far and it's cost them much to come here.'

I think of Mum and feel my face tighten.

'You've known someone who's died?' he asks.

I nod.

'Many people here believe that a person's *atman*, or spirit, lives on, even after their body is gone. They will come back in a new body. Like changing old clothes for new ones.'

'Or shedding an old snake skin for a new one,' I say, aware of the snakes still around me.

'Exactly,' he says. 'The old skin remains behind but it's empty of the snake. But the ultimate goal is to be free from the cycle of death and rebirth. And if you are cremated here, in this holy place with the Goddess Ganga, people believe that will happen.'

'What if you are cremated somewhere else – then what?'

'Then your *atman* will return to earth in another body.'

I don't believe that Mum is in a new body. I've felt her with me on the mountain. Even here, with the snakes, I know that she's still with me.

'Where did you learn to speak English?' I ask.

He smiles. 'I haven't always been a holy man.' He rests his back on the trunk of the tree, wrapping his legs around the branch he's sitting on, freeing his hands.

I realise I'm still gripping the branch with all my strength and my knuckles are turning white. I loosen my grip.

'I used to be a businessman,' he says. 'I ran a technology company in Bangalore.'

'What happened?' I ask.

He shrugs. 'I made all the money I wanted to make. What was the point of making more?'

'What's your name?' I ask.

'I gave up my name. And my old life. I'm on a constant pilgrimage now. I worship Shiva. This river, the Ganga, flows through his hair.'

My heart clenches at the idea of giving up my

life. It makes me miss Dad and Grandma. I think about how I'd give anything to have had more time with Mum, and how I wouldn't give up my family for anything.

CHAPTER THIRTY

Sleep

We sit in silence for a while, observing the water recede. As it does, it releases the stench of sewers and leaves behind a sea of debris. I pinch my nose until I grow used to the smell. I watch as washed-up boats, tyres, carts, and even dented and smashed furniture slowly become visible. A few people rummage through the rubbish. Someone helps a goat out of the tree. Eventually, I have the nerve to climb down too.

I squeeze the water from my jumper and empty my pockets. The magazine article is dripping. I think it's still legible.

'Do you know what this says?' I ask, helping the sadhu out of his tree and passing him the paper.

'Let me see,' he says, his mouth moving as he reads. 'Ah yes. *Film star Garjan Mankar has been cleared from an investigation into snow leopard poaching.*'

My heart leaps. He's due at the hotel today.

'*If you have any information regarding poaching, call this number,*' the sadhu finishes reading.

'Thanks,' I say, taking the newspaper back from him. 'Where's the train station?'

He points me in the right direction. 'Stay safe,' he says.

'You too,' I smile, press my palms together and bow, before turning and running back in the direction he said, desperate to get home quickly.

I know I'm right about the poaching now. Even the snakes in the trees felt like a message from Mum to keep going.

The trains aren't running but a kind conductor directs me to a bus. I scrabble in my pocket for the few soggy rupee notes I have and hand them to the bus conductor. Luckily it's enough and he lets me on. The bus takes hours and hours, bumping along narrow roads. I stretch, cramped in my seat. We drive alongside sheer drops and I hold my breath and squeeze my eyes shut every time we pass a car.

I think about what I'll say to Dad and Grandma when I get home. I'll show them the photographs and the article. I bite my lip. I hope it's enough to convince them that Mr Bhat and Mr Anand are poachers.

The bus stops often. Soon I'm the only person who's been on since the beginning. We wind around sharp bends, climbing higher and higher.

I keep drifting asleep and jerking back awake again. Falling asleep on a bus is my worst nightmare. What if we crash and I never wake up? My eyelids grow heavy.

At the hospital the doctor says they're going to induce a coma because of swelling in Mum's brain. They say it will give her time to heal and then she can wake up.

When I'm allowed to see her I sit on the bed beside her, holding her hand and listening to the beeps of the machines around her. I tuck her hair behind ears the way she liked it. Under all the wires monitoring her, she looks peaceful.

I tell Dad I'll stay until she wakes up.

'It will only be a few hours, right?' I say.

'It might be some days,' he replies, stroking my hair. 'You should go home with Grandma and get some rest. I'll be here.'

At home, I gather her favourite things: Caspar the snake, photos of us, her scarf, the orange marigolds from the garden. I fill her hospital room with them the next day. I know she can't see them, but I want her to feel at home when she wakes up.

We wait and wait for that moment. But she never wakes up.

The bus drives over bumpy road and I'm jolted back to the present. For months after the accident I used to stay awake and creep into Dad's room to check he was still breathing. Then I would do the same for Grandma. I'd shine the torch through my fingers to dull the brightness and watch the rise and fall of their chests.

The bus swerves around a corner. It's completely dark outside now except for the stars in the night sky and small dots of light in the distance. I have no idea where I am. I've been gone for a whole day already but in a way it feels like much longer; so much has happened. My body's stiff and tired. I pull my knees up and lean my head against the window, watching the stars above until I fall asleep.

CHAPTER THIRTY-ONE

Home

I rub my eyes and open them, immediately relieved to see the Himalayas in the distance. The sun is rising and casts a pink glow over the snowy peaks. I must have slept through most of the night. The bus ascends the windy road into the foothills and I know we're finally getting close to home. I recognise the native deodar trees whizzing by and smell the scent of pine.

After a few more hours, the bus chugs to a stop in town, in front of the dry food store and the owner with the donkeys.

I've made it.

I jump up, swing out of the bus doors and weave my way between the motorbikes, rickshaws, cars and people, until I'm on the road to Durga Mountain. I soon leave the chatter of town and the honking of horns below. Up here, it's quiet except for the thrum of cicadas and the rustle of leaves.

When the road ends, I rush up the mountain path, zigzagging around the tall trees, jumping over mossy rocks and ducking under low branches.

I go to Praveen's first. I know that Grandma and Dad will be worried, maybe angry, that I left, but I have to convince Praveen first.

I'm not sure whether Praveen will want to see me, let alone listen to what I have to say. I can still picture his angry eyes the last time we spoke. All I know is that I have to try. I owe it to the leopards.

I find Praveen hammering a panel on to the stable, the side of which is smashed open. Kuttani sits guarding beside him, ears pricked. Butterflies gather in my stomach. I take a deep breath.

'Praveen!' I call.

He turns, drops the hammer and stares at me. His expression is unreadable.

'What happened?' I ask, pointing at the broken cabin wall.

'Someone stole two goats,' he says. There's an awkward pause. 'Where have you been?' he continues. 'I thought . . .' he looks at the ground. 'Well, I thought all sorts of things.'

I explain everything to him and pull out the crumpled article and show him the photo of the tannery on my camera. 'You have to help me protect the leopards,' I say. 'Forget about Amul for now.'

'So we were right about Mr Bhat and Mr Anand,' he says. 'I'm sorry about before. I just . . . I can't believe that Amul would be involved in anything like this. But still. I'm sorry.'

I smile to myself, grateful he believes me and that we're in this together again.

Outside the hotel I take a breath, then push the gate open. Praveen follows me in.

Before we even make it two steps Grandma dashes out of the front door and squeezes me, holding me tight. She pulls back to look at me for a second before holding me close again. Tears glisten in her eyes.

'Don't you ever do that again,' she whispers into my hair.

'I'm sorry,' I say softly. 'Where's Dad?'

'Looking for you,' she says, ushering me inside. 'We searched everywhere and found your tent.' She gestures to the door and I see my tent crumpled in a pile next to it.

'We thought a bear had you until someone in town said they saw you getting on a train. Dad thought . . . he thought you might be trying to get back to Australia so he went to Delhi to search.'

'What?' I'm stunned; how could Dad think I would run off and leave them both like that? 'But what about Garjan Manka? Didn't he arrive today? Didn't Dad need to be here?'

'Oh darling, finding you is more important than greeting any hotel guest. I'd better tell him you're safe.' She strokes my hair one last time before pulling her phone out of her pocket. She speaks to Dad rapidly in Hindi.

Joey springs up to me and bounces around me. I stroke her nose.

'He wants to talk to you,' Grandma says and passes the phone to me.

'Dad?'

'Ruby!' His voice breaks. 'Are you okay?'

'I'm fine.' Guilt rips through my stomach. 'Dad? I'm so, so sorry. I can explain . . .'

'We can talk about it when I'm back — but all that matters is that you're okay, Ruby. Listen, I don't know when the next train is, so it might take me a day to get home but I'm on my way, all right? Stay put with Grandma. Ruby, I'm so happy to hear your voice. I love you.'

Grandma places biscuits on the table in front of me. I munch on them two at a time.

'Tell her about the poachers,' says Praveen. His voice is amused. 'When you've finished eating, that is.'

I make a face at him, then take a deep breath and explain everything to Grandma. I tell her about the flash of leopard skin I saw in the backpack; about following the couple on to the train, and the river breaking its banks.

She cries out at that, and presses her hands to her mouth.

'And look – I think Garjan is involved too.'

I unfold the article and hand it to her then I rest my head against the chair, suddenly too exhausted to do anything else.

The next time I open my eyes Praveen's wearing my backpack.

'Where are you going?' I ask. I must have fallen asleep. Grandma's covered me in a blanket. I push it off and stand.

'Garjan arrived this morning. He and the bosses left to go trekking a few hours ago. I'm going to find them and see what they're up to.'

My heart sinks. 'They're not trekking, they're hunting for leopards. We have to stop them.'

He nods. 'Amul's their guide,' he says through glazed eyes that tell me he still doesn't quite believe me about Amul. He shakes his head and continues. 'Whatever they're doing, I want to find out for myself. I know where they're heading. I know a shortcut and think I'll be able to catch up to them quickly.'

'I'm coming too,' I say.

'You most certainly are not,' says Grandma, bustling back into the room. 'I rang the number on the article you gave me. Someone is arriving within the next few days to investigate.'

'What if that's too late?' I ask her. 'They're hunting leopards right now.'

She furrows her brow, making deep creases

across her skin. 'If this is true, then they're dangerous men, Ruby.'

I wrap my arms around Joey. 'All the more reason to stop them,' I say.

Grandma glances at the picture of Garjun coming out of court. It's lying on the table and she reaches for it, examining the article more closely.

'How far away were they going?' she asks.

'About half a day's walk away, but I think if we take my short cut we could catch up with them within an hour or so,' answers Praveen.

She looks up at the mountains.

'Then we'd better get going.'

'You as well?' asks Praveen.

'Are you sure you want to come with us, Grandma?' I add.

'I can't let the two of you go alone,' she says. 'Besides, when have I ever turned down an adventure?'

I lunge and wrap my arms around her.

I dash upstairs to change quickly into some clean clothes. The house feels different. Empty. Suddenly I realise what's missing. I dash into my room.

'Polly?' I shout. 'Where are you?' She always greets me.

'Have you seen Polly?' I yell down to Grandma.

'She's taken herself off for a walk,' Grandma calls up. 'Don't worry — you know she always comes back.'

'Polly?' I call one last time, soothed by Grandma's words but still anxious to see her. She doesn't show.

I pack my tent, sleeping bag and torch. Just in case we need them.

Joey's snuggled up on the sofa and I kiss her goodbye on the nose. Then I grab a fleece and water bottle and join the others in the hall.

'Should we leave a note for Dad?' I ask.

'I'm sure we'll be back before him,' Grandma says, pausing in my doorway.

That's when I see she's holding a rifle. I raise my eyebrows at her.

'Just in case,' she says.

Praveen arms himself with his staff. I fasten my camera around my neck. Grandma passes me an umbrella.

We're ready.

'We've got Kuttani,' says Praveen, seeing me look around again for Polly. 'He's been this way hundreds of times with me.'

I nod and we set out, into the mountains, in search of the poachers.

CHAPTER THIRTY-TWO

Leeches

The mountain has changed in the rain; everything is heavy, dripping with moisture, extra green and wild. The clouds switch between hanging low in the sky like a fluffy sea below us and staying right on top of us like thick damp fog. The air is filled with bugs and cicadas. Orchids have blossomed and new streams flow over rocks. The ground is covered in moss and ferns, bringing shadows and earthy smells.

A big male langur sits at the top a tree, holding on to it tightly. He tilts his head back and forth, giving loud grunts and barks.

I can't see any other monkeys.

'Quickly,' says Praveen, ushering us onwards. 'It's a warning call. It means there's danger near. A bear, probably. We should pay attention.'

The monkey gives five or six more guttural barks before stopping and listening. Then he starts again.

'What do we do?' asks Grandma. 'We don't know which direction the danger's coming from.'

'We need to be loud and make noise,' Praveen tells us.

I grab a stick and bash it against trees as I pass, stomping along the path. Grandma sings in a series of la-la-las. She's still going, even when the monkey's call is far behind us.

We descend a rocky path, holding on to each

other to balance. At the bottom I notice a bunch of black worms, upright, reaching into the air like fingers from the rocks.

'That's weird,' I say, shuddering at the sight of them. Slimy things give me the creeps. 'Look at those worms.'

'They're not worms,' says Praveen. 'They're leeches.'

I freeze. That's worse than worms. Worse than slugs. One hundred times worse.

I look down and see that one has attached itself to the skin on my bare ankle.

'Get it off,' I whisper.

'You all right?' asks Praveen.

'Get it off, get it off, get it off,' I say, jumping up and down in panic.

'Hang on, hold still,' says Grandma.

I glance at it. I swear it's already growing, getting fat off my blood.

Praveen lights a match and holds the flame close to it. 'They let go if they feel heat.'

'Quickly!'

It releases and he flicks it away. It leaves a smear of blood behind.

I recoil from the sight and quickly tuck my trousers into my socks and pull my sleeves down as far as they'll go.

'Thank you,' I say.

Another leech has inched up the umbrella and

is attempting to attach itself between my fingers. I flick it off.

Grandma has her thick boots on that go halfway up her calf. I wish I was wearing some too.

'Don't worry, they're harmless,' says Praveen.

'Come on, let's go, before we get any more,' says Grandma.

I spring from boulder to boulder, eyes on the ground the whole time, dodging any leeches.

'Make sure you check your neck,' says Praveen. It sounds suspiciously like he's suppressing a laugh. 'They drop from leaves too.'

I jump, rubbing my neck and shoulders. I can't feel anything slimy, but I keep checking every few minutes, just to make sure.

We stop on the slope before we reach the bottom of the valley.

'That's the path they'll be on,' says Praveen, pointing to a rough track on the other side of the river. 'And, er . . .' he gestures to the field of stinging nettles below us. 'That's the short cut.'

I pause and glance up at Grandma next to me.

'I'm ready,' she says and rolls down her sleeves in preparation.

'Sorry,' says Praveen, sheepishly. 'I didn't realise it was so overgrown.'

Praveen leads the way, bashing a trail through the tall stingers. Grandma follows. We hold hands in a chain and lift our arms up high above the nettles.

I hear Mum's voice in my head. *This is the perfect habitat for snakes.* I picture them slithering alongside us.

I stomp my feet on the ground to scare them off with vibrations, like she taught me to.

My legs brush against the nettles and they burn. I try to ignore it.

'Not much further,' shouts Praveen from the front.

Kuttani scampers ahead and barks sharply. When we reach the end of the nettles, we see why.

A rope bridge hangs, snapped in two, one piece dangling on each side of the raging river. I look left and right but there's no other crossing to be seen.

CHAPTER THIRTY-THREE

Trekking

'When was the last time you came here?' I ask Praveen.

'Over a year ago,' he says. 'The paths are usually maintained. I guess no one comes this way any more.' His face is grim. 'I'm sorry. I made you come all this way, for nothing.'

Grandma rests on a boulder and looks into the river. Water sloshes against the bank as the current catches on stones before swirling downstream. The pebbles glitter under the water. 'Over here,' she says, suddenly. 'Look. Stepping stones.' She smiles.

I follow her gaze and, sure enough, she's right. A jagged little trail of stones punctuates the fast-flowing water.

'Are you sure we'll make it?' I ask. The stones are covered in moss and look slippery.

'I'm quite good at balancing, I'll have you know,' she says.

We leap from boulder to boulder. I go first, arms spread for balance. My heart pounds.

My right foot slips and the icy water runs over my toes, soaking my shoe.

I turn and extend my hand to Grandma to help her over the tricky bit. She holds on to me to steady herself. Her foot slides over the moss and she wobbles as she tries to find stable footing.

She starts to slip, but regains her balance and leaps on to the bank to avoid toppling into the water. She knocks into me and we tumble to the grass and sit there laughing.

I shake my foot to get the water off as Praveen crosses. Then I take a photo of Grandma and Praveen in front of the river with the stinging nettles in the background. He poses as if he's in a magazine, leaning against a boulder with his head tilted and lips pressed together in a pout.

I laugh but quickly switch the camera off. I don't want to waste the battery.

We perch on rocks and eat the chapattis Grandma has packed.

Praveen shows us a small pipe sticking out of a rock with drinking water flowing from it and we all drink thirstily. Then we set off again.

'I met a man yesterday who said the water in the Ganga was holy,' I say, suddenly remembering.

Grandma smiles. 'It does have magical properties. Your mum told me that the Ganga has a higher concentration of dissolved oxygen, which means that it has self-cleaning properties.'

'Really?' I ask. 'But it didn't look very clean. And . . . there were dead bodies in it.'

'Yes, it's too polluted now to self-clean. It's like pushing a balloon into water; when you let go it bounces back up.' She pauses. 'But if you push it deeper and deeper there will come a point where it will not bounce back by itself. That's what has happened to the Ganga.'

As she talks, we ascend into the rockier terrain. There are fewer leeches here and I'm thankful for that.

'Is there anything we can do to fix it?' I ask.

Grandma's silent for a while. 'I don't think the Ganga will ever be clean again.'

'Look,' says Praveen, bending to pick something up. 'They did go this way.'

It's a plastic water bottle and an empty instant noodle packet. Grandma shakes her head disapprovingly and puts the plastic in her bag.

I take a deep breath. We must be getting close to them now. I realise I haven't thought this far ahead.

What do we do when we find them?

CHAPTER THIRTY-FOUR

Stars

We've been walking for hours when Grandma stops at the side of the path. 'It's getting dark,' she says. 'I'm sorry, Ruby; we'll have to stop for the night now.'

'But I can tell we're right behind them,' I say. 'Let's go a bit further . . .'

'They won't keep trekking now it's getting dark,' Praveen reassures me.

I sigh. They're right. But I can't shake the feeling that we need to keep moving.

The mountains at dusk are full of buzzing insects and evening birds that flutter in and out of the trees.

We set up the tent in a grassy clearing. The sun sets in the west, bathing the line of mountains to our east in purple light. I search the horizon for signs of the poachers' fire but the slopes are still and dark. We collect fallen wood from around us and snap it, breaking it into pieces.

I arrange the kindling and light it with a match, adding bigger logs once it's caught. The smoke curls high into the sky. Yellows, blues and greens dance inside the flames.

I watch the sky change colour until stars dot the sky above us. The temperature plummets once it's dark. We sit huddled together, side by side, warming our hands and feet on the fire. My toes are still damp from earlier. I take deep breaths, tasting the wood smoke and the cold crisp air.

I stare upwards until my neck aches. I reach for my necklace.

'Are you thinking about your mum?' Praveen asks gently. 'I wanted to ask you - what happened to her?'

'She died,' I say. 'That's it.'

I catch Grandma sighing next to me.

I think about the last time we were all together as a family at breakfast on the day of the accident. Grandma and Mum were laughing about who ate the last of the jam and put the empty sticky jar back in the cupboard. They knew it was me, but they were teasing Dad.

It was nothing special. It's always felt too ordinary to have been our last morning together. There are so many things that I would have done differently.

Maybe that's why Dad wanted to leave Australia.

Maybe it was his way of saying goodbye.

'Did you know every leopard has a unique set of spots?' says Praveen.

'Like a fingerprint?' I reply.

He nods. 'I saw one once.'

'What happened?' I ask.

'It was dusk and I was near my uncle's house. I had the flock with me. It attacked them and took a sheep while I was gathering wood. Kuttani tried to fight it off.'

The dog's ears prick up at the sound of his name.

'I arrived in time to see the leopard drag the sheep into the jungle. Its body was so long and its feet were huge and padded. It moved silently.'

'Do they attack your flock often?' I ask.

He shakes his head. 'Not often — it's still pretty wild here. But the more we expand and build, the less the leopards have to eat. When they don't have enough food, that's when they'll start eating our sheep. My brother says it's already happening in other parts of India. They're venturing into cities looking for food.'

I wonder if I'll ever meet his brothers and remember Praveen telling me one's a paragliding instructor who lives in the city.

'Have you ever been paragliding?' I ask.

'Yes,' he says, and beams. 'I felt like an eagle. I'll take you one day.'

I smile.

'I'm not so sure about that,' says Grandma. 'Paragliding sounds dangerous.'

'It's safe. My brother's done it many times.'

'I think your father would want your feet to stay on the ground. As do I.'

'Grandma's scared of flying,' I lean in and whisper to Praveen.

'Oh,' he says.

I smile and lift my camera, turning the flash on to take a picture of Praveen and Grandma by the fire.

As Grandma gets up to go to bed, she trips over the pile of logs and thuds to the ground, crying out as she falls.

'Grandma,' I shout and rush towards her.

She clasps her foot with both hands.

'Are you hurt?' I ask.

'I banged my ankle against that log,' she says, rocking back and forth. 'I'm sure it will be fine in the morning.'

Later we crowd into the tent together. Me, Grandma, then Praveen. Kuttani sleeps in the porch. Grandma drifts off immediately and starts snoring. We sandwich her, lying either side.

I can't help but giggle at her snoring and Praveen laughs too. I stifle my noise by burying my head in my sleeve. I feel safe, cocooned in the vast layers of mountains.

'I'm never going to boarding school,' I whisper. 'I want to stay here for ever.

'I'd like that,' he says.

Through the darkness, I beam.

The silence fills the air around us.

'It was a car crash,' I say.

'What?'

'The way she died. My mum.'

There's a pause and then, 'I'm sorry.'

After a while I become aware of the sound of his even breathing next to Grandma's snoring. I try to stay awake, in case anything is lurking in the darkness. But my head grows heavy.

I sleep.

CHAPTER THIRTY-FIVE

Ambush

Next morning, we wake before it's light. My breath comes out in puffs of condensation and I have to rub my hands together to warm them.

While Grandma rests, Praveen and I build another fire from the leftover wood. The ash is still warm from last night and Praveen quickly boils water and makes tea. The liquid warms my insides.

Grandma climbs stiffly out of the tent. She hobbles towards us before straightening and placing her hands on her lower back.

'Are you all right, Grandma?' I ask.

'Just stiff. Give me a few minutes and I'll be fine.' She steps forwards and winces.

'Let me look at your ankle,' I say, kneeling in front of her. 'It's swollen. I think you twisted it.'

'You two should go on without me,' she says, flinching. 'I'm not sure I can walk.'

'We'll leave Kuttani with you for company,' says Praveen.

'No,' says Grandma. 'I'd much prefer you had him for safety. Make sure you're back soon though. Dad will be waiting for us otherwise.'

I pile some logs in front of her so that she can elevate her foot.

I hang my camera around my neck and Praveen picks up his staff. I pause and turn back to Grandma. 'Are you sure you'll be all right?'

I ask. I don't feel right about leaving her in the mountains all by herself.

She nods and ushers us onwards. 'No leopards are dying on my watch,' she says. 'Now, go.'

We set off with our torches. Praveen picks up pebbles and throws them along the way, to warn the bears that we're coming and scare them off.

Something skims against my leg and I jump.

'What was that?' I ask, shining the torch next to me.

Kuttani looks up at me. It was just his fur.

We walk next to each other on the thin path. Praveen's fingers brush against mine and then he clasps my hand in his. My heart races. I can't see his expression because it's dark. We walk together, hand in hand.

The tallest mountain peaks are always there in the distance. The sun rises behind them. At dawn the air fills with birds and tweets. In the growing light, Praveen spots the remains of a camp fire at the side of the path. We run and place our hands over it. It's still warm.

'We must be going in the right direction,' I say.

We walk higher and higher, climbing up to the clouds.

'My mum always says that up in the mountains there are fewer people, which means there are fewer thoughts. It's one of the reasons it's so peaceful,' says Praveen.

I'd never thought about it like that before.

The air is thinner up here. I can feel it in my chest. Abruptly, Kuttani growls and lowers his body close to the ground. I hear twigs cracking up ahead. Praveen raises his finger to his lips.

We tiptoe onwards. A smaller path has been made through the trees, off the main path. Praveen beckons me that way. I grip the camera in my hand.

Suddenly, a shot rings out into the air. It echoes off the mountains, disturbing the stillness.

I duck behind some ferns, pulling Praveen down with me. We crawl forwards on our hands and knees towards the sound. I can hear men's voices ahead. Peering between ferns, I see Toad and Stinger, and a tall man who must be the film star, Garjan Mankar.

In front of them is a leopard.

The leopard knows it's cornered and faces them snarling. Its body is low to the ground.

'Run,' I whisper under my breath. 'Why don't you run?'

But then I notice one of its back paws is stained with blood. It can only limp.

My heart leaps; it must be the same leopard I saw before.

She growls, warning them not to come closer.

It happens so fast. A click, and then the crack of their guns.

'No!' I scream.

My voice is lost beneath the sound of shooting.

And it's too late. Just like with Mum. There's nothing I can do. The beautiful leopard thuds to the ground. I collapse against a tree. And the mountains roar with me.

CHAPTER THIRTY-SIX

Leopard

The leopard lies on its stomach; a sandy-coloured coat covered in black rosettes. Its front legs are spread in front of it, with its long white tail curled round its side. The coat has a velvet sheen all over except for the bullet wound in its side. Matted blood clings to the fur.

The men tower over it, clasping their rifles. Stinger kneels, touching the leopard's fur.

'It's not a snow leopard, but it has one beautiful coat,' says Garjan admiringly. He removes his sunglasses and rests them on top of his head.

Evidence. This leopard's death can't be in vain. With shaky hands I grip the camera and switch it on. It whirs as the lens pushes out. I raise it up and focus through the leaves.

'Wait, Ruby,' whispers Praveen behind me. 'Wait—'

I press the shutter.

Click.

The air around me is bathed in bright white light as the camera flashes.

The men look up in our direction, dazed for a split second.

I forgot about the flash.

'Get back,' I say to Praveen.

Toad reacts first. He bellows and charges towards us.

In an instant, strong hands clasp around my arms, yanking me up. He tugs the camera from around my neck, breaking the strap, and hurls it against a rock. It smashes into pieces.

'No,' I say, rushing towards it. All my photos are stored on there. My photos of Mum.

Stinger heaves Praveen from the undergrowth.

'What are you doing out here?' Toad barks.

'Who are you working for?' yells Garjan, his gaze wild. 'Are you taking pictures of me?'

'We were taking pictures of animals,' I say, quickly. 'I'm practising to be a wildlife photographer.'

'I don't want to get mixed up in another scandal,' shouts Garjan to Stinger. 'You said this was safe.' He breathes heavily.

Stinger's hand hardens on my arm.

'Don't worry,' he smiles at me unpleasantly. 'These two won't be any trouble.'

Praveen is glaring at Amul, who's standing behind Toad, his eyes wide.

'Did you bring them here? Did you know they were going to do this?' Praveen asks. 'How could you, Amul?'

'The leopard killed most of my flock. I wanted it dead,' he replies, shrugging and sticking his hands in his pockets.

'We live alongside them — we always have!' Praveen shouts at him. 'You should know that!'

I can't stop looking at the dead leopard. I

wonder if it's the same one I met eyes with, that day in the jungle. The one that watched me. The one I vowed to protect. I shake Stinger off and kneel next to it, touching the soft fur, to make sure. There's no heartbeat.

'You killed it,' I hiss at the film star. 'You coward.'

His handsome face flushes red.

'I've had enough of this,' says Toad, grabbing Praveen's arms and forcing them behind his back. 'Get her!'

Stinger's hands close around my wrists.

A silhouette appears on the ridge above us. The long shape of a gun points straight towards us.

Grandma stands over us all.

'Let them go,' she calls. Her voice is calm, icy. It sends shivers down my spine.

There's a stunned silence, and then Toad laughs.

'You think we're going to believe that you, an old woman, could ever use that thing? Do you even know which end to point?'

'I'm giving you one more chance. Get away from them or I'll shoot,' she says again.

'Go and get her too,' says Toad to Stinger.

Stinger hesitates, then takes a step forward.

A bullet skims the branches above us. I can feel it whistling through the air.

'Next time I shoot, I'll be aiming for you,' Grandma says.

'Let them go,' says Garjan, stumbling backwards.

'But . . .' says Toad.

'Do what the old lady wants,' he shouts, brushing off his leather jacket.

While they're distracted, I scramble along the dirt for the camera. The blue memory card is on the ground half-hidden under some leaves. I grab it. It's cracked down the middle. I shove it quickly into my pocket.

'Go,' snaps Toad. 'But don't think you've seen the last of us.'

Grandma keeps the rifle raised, pointing at them as she ushers us behind her and backs up slowly.

'Thanks, Grandma,' I say, once we're out of sight.

'That was brilliant!' says Praveen.

'Quickly now,' says Grandma. 'We need to get back. I don't trust them one bit.'

'Wait,' I say. Kuttani has run off to the side and is barking at the hedge. 'He's found something.'

I bend down and rummage through the branches. Something scratches my wrist. I yank my hand back.

'Ouch,' I say. Then I see movement and a blur of spots. I part the foliage, more carefully this time. Two wide eyes stare back at me. A cub, falling over its hind legs as it tries to back away.

'What are you doing?' asks Grandma, urgently. 'We need to go.'

I reach forward and grab its soft warm fur.

It opens its mouth and gives a tiny roar. A high-pitched, scratchy sound.

It's calling for its mother.

It digs its claws into the earth as I reach around its body to remove it from the bush. I peer into the undergrowth to see if there are more cubs, but I can't see any, and Kuttani has stopped barking.

There must only be one.

'Is that a cub?' asks Praveen, in awe.

I nod and hide the leopard cub in the inside of my jacket to keep it calm and carry it down the slope. As I cradle the cub, my heart feels ready to burst with love for it. I know everything it's just lost.

The mountain is silent apart from howling wind.

CHAPTER THIRTY-SEVEN
Cub

We pack up the tent quickly, stuffing it all inside the backpack.

'We have to go,' Grandma says. She limps forward and groans.

'Here,' says Praveen. 'Take my staff.'

Grandma uses it to lean on and we continue down the mountain.

'How did you find us?' I ask Grandma.

'As soon as you left, my gut told me it was a bad idea to let you go.'

'But your ankle . . .'

'Some things are worth powering through the pain,' she says and reaches for my hand.

'When I was a child there were vultures everywhere,' says Praveen suddenly. 'We were frightened of them. People wanted them killed. Now they're almost all gone. They scavenged dead cattle that had been treated with medicine and it poisoned them. But now that the vultures are gone, carcasses are left to rot. Dogs get more diseases. Humans get more diseases.' He runs his hands through his hair in frustration. 'You can't just get rid of a whole species and expect it to solve all your problems. Everything's connected.'

I realise he's talking about Amul wanting to destroy the leopards.

'I'm sorry,' I say softly. 'I know he's your cousin.'

'I'm sorry I didn't believe you,' says Praveen.
'I should have.'

I smile at him.

We go the long way round downhill, bypassing the treacherous river and the field of nettles.

The cub cries and cries and my heart aches as I carry it further and further away from its mum.

'Don't worry, little one,' I whisper to it. 'I'll take care of you.'

I hum the song Mum used to sing to me, and, somewhere on the way home, it stops crying.

Dad's waiting for us when we arrive. He throws his arms around me.

'I've been so worried! What were you thinking?' He squeezes me tightly. 'Never, ever run away again. And where have you been?'

'I *didn't* run away,' I say, pulling back. When I look at his face I see he's crying.

'I thought I'd lost you too,' he says, wiping his face against his sleeve and giving me a shaky smile. He looks down at my arms and sees the leopard cub.

'What's that?' he asks.

The cub mews. Joey bounces up and sniffs it.

'Let's go inside,' Grandma says. She's been watching us with a tired smile. 'I think we need to tell Dad what's been going on.'

I tell Dad everything. About spying on Toad and Stinger, about my journey to the city, and back again, about Garjan, and about seeing them shoot a leopard dead for sport.

'The police who deal with this kind of thing are on their way,' says Grandma. 'I called them last night.'

'But we lost all our evidence,' I say. 'Unless there's something on the memory card — but it doesn't look good.' I hold out the cracked and battered memory card and try not to think of all the pictures of Mum that might be gone too.

'We need to see what's in that cabin,' says Praveen. 'There could be something in there that proves what they were doing.'

I nod eagerly. 'It's locked though.'

We follow Praveen outside. He goes to our wood pile and lifts an axe.

'Wait,' says Dad. I realise he hasn't said anything at all before now. 'You can't break in. That's their private property.'

'We have no choice,' Praveen says, carrying the axe. 'We have to get in before they get back and hide whatever's in there.' The gate swings shut behind him and he disappears down the path to the cabin.

Dad rubs the back of his head. He looks at me. 'I told you not to interfere, Ruby. Why couldn't you do as you were told for once?'

'That's not fair,' says Grandma.

I watch Dad. He doesn't seem surprised or angry about the poaching.

He seems annoyed that we found out.

'You knew,' I say quietly.

'What?' asks Grandma.

Dad shakes his head but he won't meet my eyes.

'Did you know what they were planning to do?' I ask, my voice rising.

He sighs. 'I knew they told Garjun he could hunt a snow leopard, in order to entice him to the hotel. I thought he was just some rich film star who wanted a thrill, and they were telling him what he wanted to hear. I never thought they'd actually find a leopard and kill it.'

'You saw those leopard claws at the hotel,' I say angrily. 'You knew they had rifles, hunting gear. How could you think they weren't serious? Why didn't you do anything?'

'I needed this hotel to be a success, Ruby. Not

for me – for all of us.' His voice cracks. 'The night you heard me arguing with Mr Bhat, we were arguing about Garjun coming. I told them I didn't want him to be a guest but they said I had no choice.'

'You always have a choice,' I say. 'You taught me that. You're doing the same thing as when we were in Australia, getting involved with bad people.'

'I didn't realise what they were doing, Ruby,' he replies. His shoulders drop. 'Where are they now?'

'Still in the mountains,' says Grandma. She examines Dad with piercing eyes. 'But I don't know how long we have.'

Dad nods slowly.

'Did you not hear what I said?' I ask, anger closing my throat. 'They murdered a leopard. You let them. And I'll never forgive you for that.'

I turn and run to my bedroom, leaving the cub safely there, before heading out to find Praveen.

Nerves roll through my stomach; I'll finally get to see what's inside the cabin.

CHAPTER THIRTY-EIGHT
Cabin

When I get there, Praveen is swinging the axe against the cabin door. The wood cracks. He hits it again and again and wood shards splinter into the air.

'Get back,' he says.

Thwack.

A wooden panel of the door drops to the ground, leaving a hole. Praveen sticks the axe head into the earth before pulling the sharp edges off the opening with his fingertips.

He turns on the torch and steps through the hole in the wood.

I follow him.

It's dark and Praveen shines the torch in all directions. Leopard skins hang all around us on meat hooks. Their heads and faces are still attached. Mouths open, roaring.

I retch. The bad smell I thought was rotting leaves is blood, skin and salt.

The smell of death.

Praveen inspects the skins.

'They don't have any tears on them,' he says. 'No gunshot wounds. Or knife wounds. How were they killed?'

He moves through them. There must be at least twenty in here.

Praveen shines the torch against the underside of a skin.

'It's marked,' he says. 'Look.'

I look closer and see a name stamped across the skin. But it's not Mr Bhat's or Mr Anand's. It's Rahul Veer.

Dad's name.

'They all have them,' says Praveen.

My skin tingles and I feel sick.

'I have to get out of here,' I mutter.

With a dizzy head, I step outside into the fresh air. Holding on to the cabin wall to steady myself, I double over, and vomit.

'Are you okay?' Praveen runs out after me and places a hand on my back.

I gasp that I'm fine.

'They were poisoned,' Praveen says. 'It's the only explanation.'

'How do you poison leopards?' I ask.

'You poison their food,' he says slowly.

The pieces fall into place in my mind.

'Your goats that were taken?' I ask.

He nods.

My thoughts turn to Polly. Would she eat from a poisoned carcass? I picture her lying on the ground somewhere. I have to find her.

'I'm going to look for Polly,' I say. 'I'll meet you back at the hotel.'

He nods.

'Polly!' I call, heading into the forest. I climb on top of a boulder and shout her name as loudly as I can. 'Polly!'

I wait for her bark or the rustle of the undergrowth.

Nothing.

I jog onwards, deeper into the trees.

I smell a carcass before I see it.

'Please don't be Polly,' I whisper to myself as I rush towards the putrid smell. It's been two and a half days since I've seen her.

I enter a clearing and see the carcass, dangling from a low tree branch, the head brushing against the ground. Its stomach has been slit. I cover my mouth. It's one of Praveen's goats.

The carcass is too heavy for me to take down on my own; I need help to remove it before any more innocent animals are poisoned. I rush back to the hotel and my heart stops.

Toad and Stinger are on the front porch.

Grandma and Dad are arguing with them. I hurry over.

'The police are on their way,' Dad is saying.

'That doesn't bother us,' says Toad with a nasty smile.

'It should,' I reply, striding up to them. 'I saw you shoot a leopard.'

'No you didn't,' says Toad. 'I was here the whole time. As far as I was concerned, we were running an innocent hotel.' He turns to Dad with a smirk. 'You're the one who offered to take the guest leopard hunting. You're the one who's been using the hotel as a cover to poach. Your name is even signed on the leopard skins. You're the ones who will go down for this, you and the old lady.'

I gasp. They're pinning everything on Dad. Every single detail.

'The police will believe us,' says Dad.

'Oh yeah?' says Toad, loudly. 'Who would you believe? Some children and an old lady? Or businessmen and one of the most successful film stars of all time?'

'We won't let you get away with this,' says Dad.

'What proof do you have that we had anything to do with this?' asks Toad, leaning in aggressively to challenge Dad.

Dad clenches his fists.

I think about all the times they've come in and out of the cabin. All the photos I took of them and the one of them with the dead leopard. If only the memory card wasn't broken. It's all the proof we need.

'Now call the police and tell them not to come because you made a mistake,' says Toad, thrusting his chest forward. 'Or your whole family's going to prison.'

Dad and Grandma glance at each other. Dad shakes his head desperately.

'Fine,' Dad says. 'I'll ring them.'

My throat tightens.

'Why don't you use my phone?' says Toad, passing it to him.

Dad dials the number and speaks to the police officer in Hindi.

'There. You've got what you want,' says Dad, hanging up. 'Now get out of here,' Dad yells at them. 'Now!'

Toad sniggers. 'Let's go,' he says to Stinger.

But Stinger lingers for a second, watching Dad, as if he wants to say something, before leaving.

'They poisoned a carcass,' I tell Dad shakily, as we watch them walk away. 'It's hanging in the forest — that's how they've been killing the leopards. You need to take it down. I'm worried about Polly.'

'I'll go now,' he says. 'Pack a bag, Ruby. We may have to leave again.' He takes my hand. 'And listen, I promise I never would have got involved in this if I knew the extent of it. I'll make it right again, okay? I just need time to think.'

I nod and turn to go inside. Tears gather in the corners of my eyes.

'We're not running away again,' I hear Grandma saying quietly to Dad as I go.

I step inside and wipe my face with my sleeve. I'm crying for everything. For all the loss that follows me around; for the leopard, for Polly, and for Mum. And I'm crying because I don't want to leave again. Because, despite everything that has happened, it finally feels like home here.

CHAPTER THIRTY-NINE
Polly

Later, as I'm frantically throwing clothes into a backpack, Praveen bursts through the bedroom door. Joey bounces in behind him. The skin is cut above Praveen's left eyebrow, his cheeks are flushed red and there's an anger in his eyes. 'Mr Bhat and Mr Anand are moving all the leopard skins! I tried to intervene but Mr Bhat knocked me down.'

'We have to stop them!' I say, jumping up. 'They can't get away with this.'

'It's too dangerous,' he says, shaking his head. 'When are the police coming? Are they here?'

'They're not coming,' I say and tell him about how Toad has framed Dad for everything.

Praveen sinks to the bed. 'Is that it? Are the bosses really going to get away with killing all those leopards?'

The cub mews next to him.

I stroke Joey, who nibbles my toe.

'Wait here,' I say and fetch two bottles, one for the cub and one for Joey.

We sit quietly, side by side, feeding them.

'My mum would have hated everything about this mess.'

Praveen nods. 'But I bet she would be happy about some things, like the animals you've saved.'

I smile.

'What are you going to call the cub?' he asks.

'I can't give her a name,' I say. 'It doesn't feel

right. I want to send her back out into the wild one day. What's the word for leopard in Hindi?'

'*Tendua*,' he replies.

'Then for now I'll call her Tendu,' I say.

The cub lifts her head and yawns, scrunching her eyes shut and showing rows of tiny sharp teeth.

Just then I hear it. A bark from nearby.

'Polly?' I gasp.

I cradle the cub, stand, and follow the sound with Praveen right behind me. It comes from Grandma's room but when I get there it's empty. I sit on the bed.

'Polly?' I call.

She barks from close by.

I crawl to the end of the bed and dangle my head over the side, upside down. A rough tongue licks my face. I laugh and climb down. Polly lies in Grandma's empty open suitcase under the bed. With her are three puppies.

'Polly!' I cry, letting the baby cub walk on the floor while I stroke Polly. She lowers her head and sniffs the cub, licking the cub's back like she's her own. Then she picks it up by the scruff of its neck and drops it with her puppies. She lies back down and the puppies crawl over each other to suckle. Even though the cub is three times the size of the puppies, she slots in between them and feeds too.

'I can't believe I didn't know,' I say.

'Dogs go off by themselves to have their puppies, don't they?' Praveen kneels next to me.

I nod. 'I think she's going to be Mum to the leopard cub too.' I turn and beam at him. 'This way she'll have a real shot at going back to the wild.'

We both sit and watch the puppies squeak and squirm. Their eyes are all closed.

I play with the little leopard cub like I would a kitten. She chases a piece of string back and forth, lunging for it with her big paws and batting it in the air like she's boxing. The cub rubs the side of her face against the palm of my hand. Her tail sticks straight up into the air, playfully.

A puppy rests its head on the cub's neck.

'I wish I could take photos of them,' I say. I miss my camera already.

'I can't believe you lost all your photos,' says Praveen.

I reach into my pocket and pull out the memory card. There's a crack down the middle of the plastic. I sigh. 'I don't think there's any hope of getting them back.'

'Why don't we take the memory card to the police?' asks Praveen, his eyes lighting up. 'They'll be able to salvage the photographs. I'm sure.'

I shake my head. 'What if they can't? We'd

have to tell them why the photos are important and then they might go after Dad. It's too risky.'

I look outside. It's dark and stormy.

'There's a printer's in town,' says Praveen. 'They fix cameras. We could at least try there.'

'Now that is a great idea,' I say, grinning at him. I turn the memory card over and over in my fingers. It has to work. It could be my only chance at stopping Dad from being blamed for everything.

CHAPTER FORTY

Earthquake

That evening, after midnight, the earth shakes, as if the mountain is mourning the leopard's death.

There's a deep rumbling through the ground, like a roar of thunder or a plane taking off from inside your head. I'm asleep but am jolted upright with panic. I jump out of bed and feel the ground move under my feet. The cup on the bedside table shudders on to the floor. It shakes my insides too.

The door flies open, slamming against the wall, and Dad staggers in. 'Everyone outside,' he shouts. He grabs my hand and pulls me out of bed and down the stairs. I have barely enough time to scoop up Joey. Grandma is waiting for us, clinging to the doorframe.

'Wait,' I shout, suddenly remembering Polly. 'What about Polly and the puppies? The cub?'

'They'll be all right,' says Dad.

'No!' I say and wriggle out of his grip. I leave Joey and dash back inside.

'Ruby!' calls Dad, chasing after me. 'It's too dangerous!'

Inside everything's still shaking. Plaster flakes off from the ceiling.

Polly's barking frantically under the bed. The puppies squeak. I kneel and shovel them up in my jumper with the cub. 'Let's go, Polly,' I say.

Dad catches up to me. 'Out, now!' he shouts. Half-running, half-falling, we make it outside into the garden.

And just like that, the shaking stops. Everything is still again. Dad switches the porch light on and we sit on the wall. Bugs and moths swarm around the bulb.

'A little shudder,' says Dad. 'Nothing to worry about.'

'Can I go back to bed?' I ask.

Dad shakes his head. 'There could be more. I want us outside. You can never be too careful.'

Grandma shrugs. 'If you say so,' she says, and I can tell she's upset with Dad too.

'Are you cold?' he asks us. He goes inside, returns with our blankets, and passes them to me and Grandma.

Joey pokes her head out from the pillowcase. Polly and the puppies, including Tendu, curl up together.

The air is cool and the sky clear and dotted with millions of stars. They look different here. The constellation of Orion is upside down in Australia.

For a second I think of the Goddess Durga shaking us off the mountain; but I feel this mountain in my bones and my blood, and I know the earthquake wasn't meant for me. This is where I'm supposed to be. I won't back down.

I'll stay and fight for the mountain and all the animals on it.

The toot-toot owl sounds in the distance. I find the sound comforting and wrap my blanket around me.

'How long do we have to wait out here?' I ask.

'An hour or so,' Dad says.

'Tell us the story of how you met Jean,' says Grandma.

I smile. Even though I'm still upset with Dad, this is my favourite story.

'Really?' he asks, but I can tell he's smiling too, in the dark.

'I'd like to hear it,' I say.

'Well. Your mother was working in India and staying at my hotel. I noticed her when she checked in. She laughed at something the concierge said and I immediately smiled. Her laugh was always contagious like that. One day, I was out the back of the hotel, loading up the truck with some boxes of old blankets. I was going to take them to the local shelter. Anyway, as I threw one of the boxes into the back of the truck, a baby snake went flying out of the box, squirmed in the air, and landed on my head.

I batted it away with my hand and it hit the ground and slithered off. But when I pulled my hand away I noticed two tiny puncture marks on my thumb. I'd been bitten. I had no idea how venomous it was. I honestly thought I might die.

I rushed back into the hotel to call an ambulance, and while I was on the phone with them, your mother walked in. She overheard the phone conversation and she looked straight into my eyes and the first words she said to me were, "I know what to do."

She bandaged my thumb and my arm, all the way to my elbow. "A pressure immobilising bandage," she called it. "To stop the spread of venom around the body."

"What colour was the snake?" she asked.

"Green," I replied.

"Did it have black markings on it?"

I nodded. "And yellow by its neck."

"Yellow! Are you absolutely sure?"

"Is that bad?"

Her eyes sparkled. "No," she said after a minute. "It means it was a green keelback. They're not venomous. You'll be fine."

In that moment, I knew we were meant to be together.'

Somehow, despite everything with the poachers looming over my head, I find the story reassuring. It makes me feel like Mum's close by. I yawn and rub my eyes before drifting off.

When I wake, Dad quietly says, 'I think we can go inside now and get a few hours' sleep before light.'

In my room I turn the memory card over and over in my hand. I switch on my bedside light and examine it closely. It's only the plastic casing that's cracked. Maybe, just maybe . . .

I look at the time. It's already 5 a.m. If I leave now I'll reach the market as it opens and be back by breakfast with the photographs — if the memory card still works.

I scribble a note to Praveen. I don't dare give too much information in case Toad and Stinger come back, so I write: *Gone to the market. Back soon.*

I'm prepared this time. I tuck my jeans into my socks and wear waterproof trousers over the top. There's no way leeches are getting me today.

I'm quick down the mountain, sidestepping slugs and darting down the path. The stones are slippery and I hold my arms out to balance.

It's still pitch dark. Earlier the langurs were making their warning call. There are predators out there.

A low growl.

Is it a bear?

I quicken my pace, dashing through the jungle. My feet thud on the leaves below me.

I'm almost in the town. The sun is starting to rise through the monsoon mist.

The noise from the traffic filters up into the jungle as I get closer. I emerge on to a busy street. Some people wear brightly coloured plastic ponchos. The drains overflow, sweeping dirt and rubbish along the street. The market stalls have blue tarpaulins piled up, ready to be draped over the goods if it rains.

I smell sewage pipes and car fumes. As I'm crossing the street, the clouds burst into a monsoon downpour. The streets become a sea of multi-coloured umbrellas. Rain hammers on the concrete road as I run to the photo shop. I hand over my battered memory card, explain that I need them to do what they can with it, and then wait anxiously outside under an awning. I keep glancing through the window at the assistant, willing her to hurry up.

The rain stops and people gather in the street. There's cheering and clapping in the distance. A little girl giggles and points. I follow her line of sight.

Men swathed in bright orange linen dance through the crowd, parting a path through the people. Long matted hair dangles down their backs and their faces are hidden by thick beards. They grip metal plates, holding them out to the crowd, collecting holy money. They're sadhus, like the man I met at the Ganga.

Behind them is an elephant.

It swings its trunk gently from side to side in time with its stride. Its coat is painted in bright swirls and patterns.

I gasp and step backwards, flattening myself against a shop window. It's three times my height. I've never seen an animal that big. Onlookers snap photos with their phones and I feel a sudden longing for my camera.

Rupee coins clatter on to the holy men's plates. I notice Praveen a few feet down the road watching the elephant too.

'Praveen!' I shout and wave.

He turns and spots me.

'Did you feel the earthquake?' he asks, running up to me.

I nod.

'*Durga*,' he whispers.

I keep my eyes on the elephant's swinging trunk.

'They've come from the south,' says Praveen. 'They're on a pilgrimage. It happens every year.'

The elephant is almost level with me. I catch its eye, surrounded by creases and wrinkles. Its large ear flaps as it passes, as if it's waving.

'Ready,' the shop assistant says, poking her head out of the door.

'You managed to get the photos?' I snatch them from her eagerly. 'Are they okay?'

'All fine,' she grins, handing me my memory card. 'These things are stronger than they seem.'

'Thank you,' I say, grabbing Praveen by the arm. My heart pounds with excitement. We hurry through the crowd to a little alley, and sit on a bench to look through them.

Praveen and I turn through them quickly, hunting for the one that will incriminate Toad and Stinger. The images flicker before my eyes. The Bollywood evening. The monkeys. The butterflies. The bosses coming in and out of the cabin. Grandma and Praveen by the fire.

And there it is.

The photo came out clear. The leopard is on the ground. She looks beautiful, peaceful. You wouldn't know she was dead if it wasn't for the blood.

Praveen smiles sadly. 'It's perfect. You can see their faces and everything.' He turns to me and grins. 'Just wait until the police see this.'

CHAPTER FORTY-ONE

Stinger

Two male and two female police officers in greyish-green uniforms with thick belts and matching hats are at the house when we get back, along with Toad, Stinger and Amul. One officer is taking notes while the others stand in a circle. Joey lies in the grass, sunning herself next to them.

Praveen and I glance at each other.

Dad meets me and kneels before me. 'I called the police, Ruby,' he says and sighs. 'I decided that whatever happens the only way I can make this right is if I stay and tell the truth. No more running away.'

'Dad,' I whisper. 'I have proof it wasn't you that killed those leopards.'

At the same time as I'm whispering to Dad, Amul speaks up, 'I swear it was those two,' he says, pointing at the bosses. Dad looks over at Amul and doesn't hear me.

'He's their friend,' replies Toad. 'Of course he's going to say that.'

'And where are these leopard skins that incriminate Mr Veer?' asks an officer with a moustache, pointing at Dad.

'I have one here,' says Toad, strutting forward and opening his backpack. 'I wanted to make sure he didn't destroy the evidence.'

'Liar,' I shout.

Toad glares at me and lifts a leopard skin out

of the bag. He shows the officer the name written on the underside of it.

'Is this your name?' the officer asks Dad.

'Yes,' Dad nods. 'But I didn't do this. I've never even seen this before. I'm the one who rang you.'

'We'll need to ask you further questions,' replies the officer, holding out a pair of handcuffs.

'Wait!' I say. 'It wasn't him.' I look around at everyone's faces. 'I can prove it.'

I show the officer the photograph. 'See,' I say. 'My dad wasn't there. It was Mr Bhat and Mr Anand.'

Stinger shifts from foot to foot and sighs.

The officer nods at the other two standing police and they step forwards.

'Mr Bhat,' the woman says, stepping towards him. 'You're going to have to come with us.'

Toad turns a deep red. 'You've got nothing on me. Some kids and one photograph. That proves nothing.' He spits out his words.

'I'll confess,' says Stinger, quietly.

'What are you talking about?' asks Toad.

'I'll confess,' Stinger repeats, looking between Dad and Grandma. 'It was us. We've been poaching leopards for months. The hotel was a front.'

'Shut up!' Toad cries. 'You're going to ruin everything!'

Stinger nods. 'I'm tired. I've had enough of this all. I used to protect animals like this one here.' He points at me. 'Not poach them.'

'Do you know how long it's taken me to make everyone believe that stupid curse here to keep people away? I even had to start a fire!' Toad says.

The police step towards him.

'Well I'm not going down alone,' Toad yells and he makes a sudden lunge for Joey.

Kangaroos can't hop backwards and Joey trips as she turns to get out of the way. Toad grabs her.

'No!' I shout, charging at him.

It's too late. His arms are wrapped Joey's neck. He's strangling her.

Dad dives at him and grabs Toad's arms, forcing them apart.

Joey wriggles out of his grip but Toad seizes her leg again.

The police tackle Toad. Joey is there, under a tangle of arms and bodies. I edge closer, trying to spot a way to get Joey free. Kangaroos scare easily. They can die from fright.

'Stop it,' I scream, louder than I ever knew was possible. They pause for a second.

'Let her go,' I say.

And just then, as everything hangs in the balance, something drops from the doorway on to the ground.

'Snake!' Praveen shouts.

Toad jumps and backs away.

Caspar the taxidermy python lies on the ground.

Polly comes leaping out of nowhere. She must have heard me cry. She snarls, leaps up and bites Toad's arm.

'Argh!' he says, letting go and grabbing his arm.

Everyone falls back.

Joey lies on the ground, panting. Her little chest rises and falls too quickly.

I rip my jumper off, cover her eyes, scoop her up, and hold her to my chest.

I turn to Stinger and Toad. 'The world isn't yours to take without thinking about others,' I say. 'You can't just hurt living things to get what you want. I know that. And I'm twelve.'

I carry Joey to my bedroom. 'You're going to be fine,' I whisper soothingly. 'He's gone now. The danger's gone.'

I kiss her head and lay her in her hanging pillowcase pouch. I want to cuddle and hug her but I know that could make it worse. All I can do is make sure she's in a quiet, warm place.

I watch from the window as Toad and Stinger are marched off the mountain.

The police officer opens my bedroom door. 'Knock, knock,' she says. 'Is the animal going to be all right?'

'I hope so,' I say and shrug.

'Did you take the photographs?'

I nod.

'I've been trying to uncover this poaching ring for years,' she says. 'They have hotels as fronts all over the mountains. You saved a lot of animals. Well done, Ruby.'

She smiles and leaves.

The door opens again, and Praveen enters. I turn away from him and wipe my face with my sleeve. I gulp and turn back towards him, grateful the light is dim. I raise my finger to my lips and point at Joey.

'Is she okay?' he whispers.

'I don't know,' I say, and my voice cracks.

He sits on the edge of the bed next to me and we stay there for a while, quietly watching Joey together.

Joey doesn't come out for the rest of the day. I keep checking on her to make sure she's still breathing. I don't let Polly come in and see me, even when she paws at the door, in case Joey feels scared.

Later, Grandma brings me fresh papaya cut

into slices. 'Why don't you play with the puppies or go outside and get some fresh air?' she says, as I nibble on the fruit. 'You've been in here for hours. I'll look after Joey for a bit. Praveen and Amul are outside talking to your dad.'

'Okay,' I say listlessly and amble outside. I pass Amul's bag on the way to the garden. It must have got knocked over in the commotion. A giant torch has rolled out of it and I notice it's got a film on it. A green filter. I frown and switch it on under my jumper. It looks like the lights. The flickering lights from Durga.

'Amul?' I shout. He stops when he sees me with the torch.

'What's that?' asks Praveen, who has turned at my shout. He sees the torch too. 'You were the lights?' he asks Amul.

'Mr Bhat paid me to do it,' Amul answers. 'I tried to say no but he threatened me.'

'But . . . how?' asks Praveen.

'People already believed in the lights from the legend. All I had to do was make sure the torch was switched on by nightfall.'

I don't even want to hear about it, I realise; it doesn't matter any more, not now Joey is in danger. I leave them and go and sit on the wall and hug my knees, listening to the breeze rustle through the pine trees and watching the butterflies.

Footsteps approach behind me.

'Can I join you?' asks Dad.

I nod.

Dad sits next to me on the wall.

I shift my position and swing my legs over the side.

'I'm sorry, Ruby. I was so desperate for this to work that I ignored what was going on right in front of me.'

I'm quiet.

'Your mum was always the strong one, you know,' he says finally. 'And I know I've done a terrible job of stepping up, but I'm determined to do better from now on. I still want to make a success of this hotel, if you want to stay?'

I smile and nod, flooded with warmth.

'We could organise wildlife photography courses up here. What do you think?'

'That sounds good,' I reply.

'You know, I see your mum in everything around us,' he says, patting the wall. 'Like this wall . . . it reminds me of the time we climbed over a wall into a Maharaja's garden in search of a snake.'

'You don't talk about her much any more,' I say, my voice wavering slightly. 'It makes me feel like we're forgetting her.'

'I know. I think I've been too ashamed of what she'd think of me right now,' he replies. 'Your mum lives on in you, Ruby. She would be so proud of what you did today and how you saved the cub.'

I smile. I know he's right. I can feel it in my bones.

That night, as I curl up with the leopard cub, I realise I'm not afraid any more.

I'm not scared of the dark, or of falling asleep. Going through everything I did to save the leopard made me realise I can handle more than I thought. The prospect of car crashes makes me nervous, but there's still time to work on that one. I roll over and listen to the gentle squeak of Joey's breathing from the corner of the room. Outside, an owl calls. The shadow of Georgie and her eight legs crawls along the ceiling above me. I fall asleep clutching my necklace, and dream of Mum.

EPILOGUE

Two weeks later, Praveen and I are lying on rugs on the veranda outside, next to the orange lilies. It's the middle of monsoon and we're surrounded by a cloud that drifts inside if we leave a window open.

The puppies have found their feet and Polly has brought them out. They clamber all over us, wagging their tails. The cub is among them. She wiggles her bum and pounces on me with a tiny roar. I stroke her soft pelt and she rubs my cheek with her nose in return.

Dad has framed my photographs of the firefly tree, the langurs and the butterfly migration, and hung them on the wall. There's also a framed newspaper article. We made the national news.

'I've got it,' calls Amul, appearing round the corner.

I sit up. He carries a piece of thick paper and a pen. Printed on the paper are the words:

I do solemnly declare to be a protector of the mountain and a watcher of the wild.

He signs underneath before passing the pen to me. I write my name, and then Praveen does. Together we hang it on the wall, next to the newspaper article.

'Ruby?' calls Grandma.

She bustles through the door carrying Joey,

who leaps out of her arms and into mine.

'She left the pouch for the first time by herself!'

I hug Joey, stopping myself from squeezing her too tightly.

'I knew you'd recover,' I whisper to her and she licks my nose. 'You're tougher than you look.'

Just like me.

Poaching Ring Uncovered

A poaching ring has been uncovered by a local boy and girl on Durga Mountain. The authorities have been after the mastermind responsible for poaching operations up and down the country for seven years. A total of 40 leopard skins and 120 leopard claws have been seized.

Celebrity Garjan Mankar was also arrested, although the extent of his involvement is still unknown.

Mr Anand agreed to testify against the ring leader, Mr Bhat. He said Mr Bhat went to great lengths to keep people away from the areas he wanted to poach in, including committing arson. Mr Anand used to work in a wildlife reserve, preventing poaching, when his daughter fell ill and he needed extra money for hospital bills. 'The poachers were getting more money than me,' he says. 'I didn't feel like I had much of a choice.' After that, he became involved with Mr Bhat's operations.

The hotel that was being used as a front for their illegal activities is being transformed into a wildlife centre in an attempt to spread awareness of the unique wildlife on the mountain. The founder, Rahul Veer, commented, 'My late wife, Jean, dedicated her life to the conservation of animals, particularly snakes, and the centre will be named after her.'

Author's Note

In the 1960s my Grandma and Grandpa travelled by boat and overland from Australia to India. They took with them their four sons, a border collie dog called Polly and a kangaroo joey.

Eventually they settled on a foothill in the Himalayas, which is the setting for *When the Mountains Roared*. While they were living there, my uncle rescued an abandoned leopard cub and cared for it until it was old and strong enough to be released back into the forest.

I spent much time in India as a child and many of Ruby's animal encounters are based on my own memories from my Grandma's house there: the scorpions creeping out of the fireplace, the bear scratching at the door to get the dog food and the leeches inching up Ruby's leg.

I grew up listening to my Grandma talk about her adventures in India, the mountains she loved and the wildlife she discovered there. She passed away as I was writing this book but though she's no longer here to tell those stories, they live on in my memories and my writing. She'll always be the one who introduced me to the wonder of the Himalayas with its annual butterfly migration, its forests full of bears, leopards and langur monkeys, and its native red-flowering rhododendron trees. It's an honour to be able to share her stories.

Wildlife conservation is something very close to my heart and nowadays we understand the many negative impacts of removing live animals from their endemic countries, which include damage to animal welfare and risk of invasive species. Under no circumstances should you ever attempt to smuggle a kangaroo out of Australia.

Acknowledgements

To everyone at Orion, thank you for turning *When the Mountains Roared* into this beautiful book and sending it out into the world.

To my fantastic editor, Lena McCauley, thank you for all your hard work and editorial input, and your patience and trust when suddenly writing felt tougher after my Grandma died.

To my agent extraordinaire, Sallyanne Sweeney, for all your comments, suggestions and your continued guidance and support. Thank you.

To Genevieve Herr, thanks for your wonderful edits and thoughts.

Fliss Johnston, thank you for knowing I wanted to write this book before I did.

To Rob Biddulph, for such a gorgeous cover. It couldn't be more perfect. Thank you! And to Thy Bui for putting the designs together.

To Jason Cohen for my author photograph.

To Steph Allen and Dom Kingston for organising and accompanying me on exciting adventures to schools, festivals and studios.

A huge thank you to all the booksellers, reviewers, bloggers, teachers and librarians who have championed *Running on the Roof of the*

World. I'm honoured to be part of this inspiring community.

To my workshop crew: Jennifer, Sarah, Alyssa, Irulan, Carlyn, Mel, Jas, Tracy, Wendy, and Miranda.

To the Bath Spa MA in Writing for Young People alumni, thank you for your continuing support. You are a special bunch.

Thanks also to the authors who have been so supportive, including David Almond, Sophie Cleverly, Christopher Edge, Abi Elphinstone, Sarah Driver, Kieran Fanning, Claire Fayers, Julia Green, Mimi Thebo, Steve Voake and Amy Wilson.

To everyone who let me write in their house as I moved between countries: Pine Cottage, Hotel Eagles Nest, Basunti, Jemima's, Granny Mary's, Anne and Rick's, Mum's, Aunty Jo's, Emma's, Kim and Hazel's. This book was written over three continents which I think fits the story perfectly.

To Uncle Kim, for putting up with all my questions and for rescuing a leopard cub in the first place.

To Mum, Granny Mary, Anne and Rick, Dan K, thank you for all your love and support.

To all my friends and family on both sides of the pond. My sisters, Rachel, Olivia and Hazel. Emma, Fran, Nick, Dan, Louise, Alex, Anna,

Dave, Jake, Louise, Cassie, Jamie, Angelica, Rogier, Kate, Emily and Jon J.

To Dad, for taking me trekking in the Himalayas as a child.

To everyone on the mountain. It will always have a special place in my heart.

To my husband Jonathan, who I met there.

Jess Butterworth spent her childhood between the UK and India, and grew up hearing stories about the Himalayas from her grandmother. She's lived in India and even met with the Dalai Lama. She studied creative writing at Bath Spa University and now lives in Louisiana, USA.